The Philosophical Detective

Also by Bruce Hartman:

Perfectly Healthy Man Drops Dead

The Rules of Dreaming

The Muse of Violence

The
Philosophical
Detective

The True Story of an Imaginary Gentleman

by

Bruce Hartman

Swallow Tail Press

Published by Swallow Tail Press
Philadelphia, PA, USA
www.swallowtailpress.com
Not for sale outside the United States of America

ISBN-10: 0988918129

ISBN-13: 978-0-9889181-2-2

"CLUE®" is a registered trademark of Hasbro, Inc.

The cover art is a detail from William Blake, *The Body of Abel Found by Adam and Eve,* in the Tate Gallery, London. The fleeing figure is Cain.

Author's Note

This is a work of fiction. Any resemblance to actual events or persons, living or dead, is entirely coincidental. I need hardly add that "Jorge Luis Borges" is a purely fictional product of my own imagination, not to be confused with the famous Argentine writer of the same name. I apologize in advance for taking these liberties with the reader's expectations.

1.

Murder Considered As One of the Fine Arts

> Now, if merely to be present at a murder fastens on a man the character of an accomplice,—if barely to be a spectator involves us in one common guilt with the perpetrator; it follows of necessity, that, in these murders of the amphitheater, the hand which inflicts the fatal blow is not more deeply imbrued in blood than his who sits and looks on....
>
> Thomas De Quincey, "On Murder Considered As One of the Fine Arts" (quoting Lactantius)

I met Jorge Luis Borges soon after he arrived at Harvard to deliver the Charles Eliot Norton Lectures in 1967. He was already an old man, enjoying belated renown as a poet, essayist and short story writer, though he had many more years to live. I was young, a first-year graduate student in Comparative Literature at Ipswich University, twenty miles north of Cambridge. Until then I had only vaguely heard of Borges. All I knew was that he came from Argentina and had been known to write reviews of nonexistent books; he was obsessed with labyrinths and—most unusual in a blind man—he had a deathly fear of mirrors. The circumstances of our first encounter couldn't have been more mundane. One morning my faculty advisor, Cliff Jensen, asked me to drive to Cambridge and pick up Borges and his wife for a reception at the home of our department chairman, Howard Vaughan. Cliff was a great teacher and mentor, and like all his students I would have done anything he asked. He chose me because I spoke a little Spanish and had an old Ford Galaxie that would be perfect for transporting a pair of elderly strangers from a strange land.

Their apartment in Cambridge was smaller and shabbier than I'd expected. But surroundings meant nothing to Borges, since he was blind. He insisted on speaking English, ignoring his wife except for social formalities. He was tall and aristocratic, balding under a thin halo of gray hair. His gaze was abstract, otherworldly, often astonished, like the mirrors he abhorred. He wore a charcoal gray suit and a silk tie, and he carried an ivory-handled walking stick. His wife was short, cylindrical and humorless, as befits a Latin American matron of a certain age. In the car Borges spoke excitedly of H.P. Lovecraft, whom he apparently expected to meet in Ipswich. He thanked me for "rescuing" him from Harvard, where he'd been accused of spending too much time visiting other colleges and New England literary sites. I'd be seeing him again, he said—he'd agreed to conduct a seminar at Ipswich a few weeks later.

I parked in front of Howard Vaughan's handsome colonial house and escorted the old couple inside at a pace that would have been excruciating for a snail. In the spacious entry hall, we were met by an obsequious posse of graduate students and junior faculty; there was a great deal of bowing and scraping, invisible to Borges and incomprehensible to his wife. Borges allowed no pictures to be taken, on this or any other occasion—he regarded photography as an abomination akin to mirrors. He spoke of his admiration for Lovecraft and made a few references to Emerson and Poe. Señora Borges spoke in phrases memorized from an archaic Berlitz guide. "How do you do?" she asked everyone. "Enchanted to have made your acquaintance."

In the living room, a lively cocktail party was under way. Borges, propped on his walking stick, asked me not to leave his side. I guided the couple to a small sofa and introduced them to Cliff Jensen and one of my fellow graduate students, Marty Levin. Cliff, my advisor, was the most likeable man I'd ever known, with lank blond hair, bright blue eyes, and a smile as wide and open as the Midwestern sky. He hailed from Iowa, where friendliness and optimism are apparently grown by the bushel along with the corn. Marty was a New Yorker with a dark curly beard, and as thoughtful and generous a man as I'd ever known. He was a little older than me and had gone out of his way to show me the ropes when I arrived at the university. Marty was a specialist in fantastic literature and he seemed especially eager to meet Borges. We were soon joined by Howard's ungainly seventeen-year-old daughter Clarissa, who looked and sounded like a boy.

"Cliff is the most accomplished scholar at the university," I told Borges. "He's read everything that's ever been written."

Borges muttered something about the inexhaustibility of literature and asked Cliff: "Then you are the head of the department?"

Cliff blushed in embarrassment. He'd been Howard's loyal lieutenant for over twenty years—the only member of the department who could stand him—and Borges's question must have sounded blasphemous. "That'll never happen!" he laughed.

"Why not?"

"Howard will never retire." Cliff pointed toward a circle of sycophantic students near the fireplace. "Would you, if you were lord of all you surveyed?"

In the middle of the group stood Howard Vaughan— red-faced, white-bearded, ill-tempered and half-crocked— pontificating to his disciples. He'd studied at Oxford, written novels, poems and plays, lectured in Ireland on Joyce and Yeats, summered on Mallorca with Robert Graves, debated politics with Susan Sontag and Hannah Arendt. But none of his attainments seemed to have done him any good. He was a liar, a cynic, a bully and a sexist (a word we didn't yet have, but it would have fit him). Even as he brayed on about D. H. Lawrence he had his hands all over one of the female graduate students, Rachel O'Meara, who didn't exactly leap away. After all, he was head of the department.

Rachel was the new excitement in our world, a long-stemmed Irish rose with ice-blue eyes and a lilting Sligo brogue. When she arrived from Ireland, Howard had asked me to pick her up at Logan Airport; I agreed but then foolishly inveigled a graduate student from Germany, Michael Koch, into taking my place. To my chagrin, Michael had Rachel in the sack almost before they made it back to Ipswich. Naturally I was envious—all the men in the department were envious—of the tall, athletic-looking Michael Koch, with his Germanic self-assurance and cheerful good looks. And I felt his pain, now that Rachel was rumored to be two-timing him with Howard Vaughan.

"Rachel and Howard have a history," Cliff told Borges, "that goes back twenty years. Howard was teaching at the Yeats Summer School in Sligo and had a drunk driving accident, killing a couple of people including Rachel's older brother. It was a nightmare—I had to go over there and deal with the police and the lawyers. They could have hanged him but he pulled some strings and got off with a huge fine. Rachel was just a child at the time. Years later, he went back to lecture in Dublin and met Rachel—"

He caught himself when he realized that Howard's daughter was listening.

"Go ahead," Clarissa said. "I've heard it all before."

"Well," Cliff hesitated, "without going into the details, he invited her to come here to study when she finished her degree."

"And the first thing she did," Marty grinned, "was hop in bed with Michael Koch."

Clarissa rolled her eyes. "And the second?"

Rachel's revived romantic interest in Howard seemed to be common knowledge, except to Michael Koch. He pushed his way into the circle and merrily tried to pry her away from Howard's grip. "Come on, old man! Ha! You must learn to keep your hands to yourself!"

Howard's wife, Margaret, seized this moment to swoop in and pluck his drink from his hand—"Now, Howard! You've had quite enough!"—but when she stepped away, he ordered Clarissa to fetch him another from the kitchen. Clarissa complied, though not without an obscene gesture, unnoticed by her father, followed by a conspiratorial smirk at Marty, who burst out laughing. Cliff and I laughed too, and Margaret silenced us with a withering scowl. Borges—whose wife whispered into his ear in Spanish—was not amused. Everyone knew Howard was an ass, but, like the New England weather, nobody did anything about him.

If anyone could handle Howard, it was Margaret. She was taller than he was and outweighed him by fifty pounds. She'd been a beauty in her day, people said, and you could still see a glimmer of it in her lively dark eyes when she smiled. But after twenty years of being walked on and cheated on by Howard, of covering up for Howard and apologizing for Howard, she'd been twisted (the same people said) into a dark mirror image of Howard at his worst. Clarissa was their only child.

When Clarissa returned with Howard's drink, Margaret intercepted it and offered it to Señora Borges. "God damn it!" Howard exploded. "Can't a man even get a drink in this country?" His eyes fixed on Cliff. "Jensen! Get me a drink! I don't give a good goddam what Mother Superior says!"

Margaret glowered at Cliff. "Don't you dare!"

I could feel Cliff wilting beside me.

"All right, then. Marty!"—Howard shook his finger at Marty, who moonlighted as Howard's lackey when Cliff was unavailable —"You get me one! There's a bottle of Johnny Black on the kitchen table."

"Have you known Howard a long time?" I asked Borges.

"We were recently introduced," he frowned. "Evidently by one of my enemies."

Cliff flashed one of his famous smiles. "I hope you're planning to come back for the seminar. The choice of topic is entirely up to you."

"I've already selected a topic," Borges said. "Inspired by one of my favorite writers, Thomas De Quincey."

"His essay on opium addiction?"

"No. A different essay: 'On Murder Considered As One of the Fine Arts.'"

A few days later Borges summoned me to his apartment. He greeted me warmly and explained why he'd asked me to come. Harvard University, he said, had dispatched a battalion of students, teaching assistants and would-be translators to pester him and keep him from leaving the campus. He felt trapped in his apartment and missed his old haunts in the back streets of Buenos Aires. I told him about a Portuguese coffee shop in Somerville where they served maté from southern Brazil and his face lit up with an almost childish delight. His wife, he said—she sat grimacing uncomfortably on the sofa—preferred to stay at home by herself. "And you and I have work to do," he said, reaching for his walking stick. "We must prepare for our seminar."

Borges loved the Iberian atmosphere of the coffee shop and he loved to talk. He talked about literature, philosophy, politics—each with a curiously archaic flavor, since his access to the written word had ceased when he lost his sight in the early 1950s. Inevitably the conversation came around to Howard Vaughan, whom Borges despised. Beyond merely disliking him—which was a common enough reaction—Borges viewed him as a monster and an affront to everything he held dear. "The man has read all the books," Borges said, "even written a few, and yet he is a buffoon and a moral pygmy. How can that be? Is literature just a game, like playing cards, that can be played equally well by a scoundrel or a saint?"

"Howard is definitely something of a scoundrel," I said, dodging the question.

"I take that personally, since he claims to have studied my work. Did he learn nothing from it?"

Borges's indignation caught me by surprise. Admittedly I still hadn't read any of his work, but I had the impression that it was rather cerebral and tended more toward the aesthetic than the moral. "Do you regard yourself as a moralist?" I asked him. "I thought—"

"My work is literary and aesthetic, and therefore profoundly moral in nature."

I nodded uncomprehendingly.

"What is always omitted from a word or any other symbol?" He answered his own question: "The thing that the symbol refers to. For that reason art—though it concerns itself only with balance and order and symmetry—is always about justice and morality."

I gestured to the waitress—a dark-haired beauty about my age—for a refill of my coffee and Borges's maté. This beverage, which I had never seen before, is a kind of tea that is sipped through a metal straw from a cup made from a calabash gourd. The waitress winked at me as she poured more hot water into Borges's cup. I assumed that she had overheard our conversation.

Borges stirred the metal straw around in his cup and went on: "If two brothers, starting on the day they were born, read all the same books in the same order, they would have the same ethics. In a moral sense they would be the same man. You or I, depending on the syllabus, might be Howard Vaughan. Cain might be Abel."

"Those two didn't turn out the same," I observed.

"Regrettably they had no books. You'll recall that their parents had just been driven from Paradise."

On that note we began work on the syllabus for "our" seminar—somehow I'd been drafted into doing most of the work. We met every day for a week in that coffee shop in Somerville. I took notes and read aloud to Borges to refresh his recollection of important texts (which was mostly unnecessary: he could quote long passages verbatim from books he'd read forty years before). The topic, as he'd told Cliff Jensen, was "On Murder Considered As One of the Fine Arts," based on the De Quincey essay. The syllabus included some classic texts—the *Oresteia*, passages from Dante, and of course *Crime and Punishment*, *Hamlet* and *Othello*. But our starting point, as he'd hinted, was just outside the Garden of Eden. "The first murder in literature is the story of Cain and Abel," he told me that first day. "It's the earliest murder mystery, and it's a chilling one because it's about a motiveless crime. No motive is necessary—we're within living memory of Adam's Fall. Imagine the horror Cain must have felt when he discovered the demon of evil for the first time—in his own heart. Today this strikes at our vanity as human beings. We insist on a motive. We don't like to think of ourselves as naturally evil."

He took a sip of his maté and went on: "And so in literature our murders must have strong, clear motives. Othello is driven by jealousy; Clytemnestra slaughters Agamemnon to avenge her daughter's sacrifice. In modern times, when men are no longer ruled by destiny, we find a character like Raskolnikov, whose motive for killing is nothing more elevated than financial gain. To Aeschylus and Sophocles such a crime would not have been worth writing about, even if the killer had the noblest of self-delusions. But for us, psychology has replaced divine command; we believe in psychology in the same way the ancients believed in destiny. And we believe that it excuses our fascination with the meanest of crimes."

Borges and I worked on our syllabus until there was nothing left to say on the subject of murder. It all seemed academic, just a literary exercise. I turned in the syllabus; the department posted notice of the seminar. A big turnout was expected.

And then Howard Vaughan was found dead in his home. He'd been stabbed in the back with a kitchen knife as he sat at his desk.

I telephoned Borges immediately with the news.

"The wife's been arrested," I told him. "Margaret. Apparently she caught him writing a love letter to Rachel O'Meara."

"The Irish girl? I remember her voice: deep and musical. Does Margaret admit that she killed him?"

"No, of course not. She's got a fancy lawyer and they're denying everything. She claims she came home and found him dead."

"And what did the letter say?"

"He'd started to address it to Rachel, didn't even finish writing her name—"

"What? What did he write?"

"Just the first few letters: R-A-C-H-E."

Borges hooted like a small boy enjoying a joke. "R-A-C-H-E? And on this basis they arrested the wife? Don't the police in this country read Sherlock Holmes?"

The next morning brought balmy weather—a pleasant surprise in that harsh season—and Borges insisted that we sit outdoors, on a bench overlooking the Charles River. He seemed lost in thought. "If Howard Vaughan's wife didn't kill him," he finally asked, turning to me with his glassy stare, "then who did? What was the motive?"

I had hoped we could talk about something other than the murder. On that subject I was the bearer of bad news from the department: under the circumstances, a discussion of "Murder Considered As One of the Fine Arts" would be in extremely poor taste. Borges's seminar would have to be canceled.

"According to Margaret's lawyer," I stalled, "the motive was theft. Howard was editing an anthology of student writing and the manuscript had been sitting on his desk. Margaret says that when she found the body, the manuscript was gone."

"What else was on the desk?"

"Just a couple of books. A poetry anthology—it was open to 'The Waste Land.' You know, T.S. Eliot."

Borges nodded excitedly. "Rachel is Irish, of course. At the reception she was with a young German, I recall."

"Michael Koch."

"'*Mein Irisch Kind, wo weilest du?*—Where do you linger, my Irish child?' I'm sure you recognize that line from 'The Waste Land?'"

"Sure," I lied.

"It's originally from *Tristan und Isolde.*" Borges turned his sightless eyes toward a rowing team that skittered over the river like an insect. "At the reception, I heard the story about Howard Vaughan killing Rachel's brother in Ireland and then Rachel falling in love with the man who'd been sent to bring her to Ipswich. That's more or less what happens in *Tristan und Isolde.* The reference could hardly be coincidental."

"You think Rachel killed Howard?"

He ignored my question, jabbing his walking stick into the gravel in front of the bench. "What was this missing manuscript?"

"Just an anthology of student writing. It wasn't worth anything."

"Then who would kill for it?"

I felt a little sick when he said that. "There's something you might as well know," I said, "since everyone else does. Marty Levin—you met him at the party—submitted a story that was selected for the anthology. Afterwards he tried to withdraw it, and Howard wouldn't let him. They got into an argument over it at one of our departmental meetings."

"Why would Vaughan refuse to take the story out?"

"Howard was like that. He liked to lord it over people who were in his power. He tried that with me and when I resisted he threatened to throw me out of the program."

"Didn't you say there was another book on the desk?"

"Yes, a collection of stories by the German writer Hoffmann. Nobody knows what it was doing there."

"'Mademoiselle de Scudéry!'"

"Excuse me?"

"I'll wager that the collection includes a story called 'Mademoiselle de Scudéry.' It's about an artist named

Cardillac who crafts beautiful jewelry to sell to rich aristocrats and then murders them to retrieve his creations. You see, Cardillac is an artist and his works are his children. He can't bear to part with them. Like your friend Marty Levin."

"Marty wouldn't kill anybody. And he didn't even write that story. He sent it in as a prank."

"A prank?"

"That's what he said. Cliff and I took Marty out for a beer and razzed him about the story after that argument with Howard. He got really upset and insisted he didn't write it, but he refused to say who did, and he wouldn't tell us what it was about. He said he was sworn to secrecy."

"Obviously," Borges smiled, "there's more here than meets the eye."

I stood up and helped him to his feet. "Listen," I said, "I've got to tell you something. The seminar has been canceled."

He snatched his hand away. "Nonsense!"

"No, really." I steadied him on his walking stick. "Once there's been a real homicide, you can't go around talking about murder as one of the fine arts."

"Of course you can! Literature is not a game."

The seminar would never have taken place but for a twist of fate that no one—except possibly Borges himself— could have foreseen. Three days later Marty Levin fell, or was pushed, off the roof of his apartment building. The coroner ruled it suicide, but the *Globe* called for an investigation. Borges, who'd spent much of his life standing up to the dictator Perón, was not one to be trifled with. He threatened to hold a press conference and call for an international boycott of the university if he was denied the right to proceed with his seminar.

The department (thanks to Cliff Jensen, who was now acting chairman) quickly reversed itself and agreed to hold the seminar. Borges and I met one last time to discuss some additions to the syllabus—"A Study in Scarlet," "The Waste Land," *Tristan und Isolde*, and "Mademoiselle de Scudéry," along with *Macbeth* and *Richard III*—and to review the latest developments in what he called "the case." By this time Margaret had been released on bail, and her lawyer was pointing the finger at poor Marty Levin, who wasn't around to defend himself. At a hearing shortly before Marty's death—which Marty did not attend—the attorney had all but accused Marty of the murder. Margaret testified that she'd read the missing manuscript, including the story Marty had submitted: it was a Kafkaesque fantasy about a professor resembling Howard who torments the people around him in his careless, mean-spirited way until finally his victims have him arrested, tried and executed. Howard had been furious about the story, Margaret said, and that was why he refused to let Marty withdraw it from the anthology. Borges questioned me closely about the newspaper coverage, asking me several times if the police had found the manuscript in Marty's apartment (they had not). I didn't understand why Borges thought that was even a possibility. As I reminded him more than once, Marty told me he didn't write the story. The notion that he'd killed Howard to retrieve it was absurd.

Borges had little to say on the drive up to Ipswich. We arrived at Hathorne Hall and proceeded to the auditorium at the pace of a Galapagos tortoise. Cliff had three chairs set up on the dais, one for Borges, one for himself and one for me in my new role as seeing eye dog. I parked Señora Borges in the first row, where she assured a steady stream of well-wishers that she was enchanted to have made their acquaintance. Then I guided Borges to his seat on the dais and stood behind him as an eager crowd pressed forward to greet him.

To everyone's surprise, Margaret walked in with her daughter Clarissa, both of them wearing black. Margaret tried to prove her innocence by hugging the professors' wives and repeating the testimony she'd given at her bail hearing. Clarissa looked out of place in a dress. She clung to her mother's side, her eyes bloodshot, her complexion blotchy. As she stepped up to greet Borges she started to say something about Marty, but her mother cut her off— "Some people care more about the murderer than his victim," Margaret said—and pulled her away, almost colliding with Rachel O'Meara and Michael Koch. Those two were an item again. Margaret seemed scandalized that her husband's mistress had taken a new lover so quickly.

Cliff stood up and asked everyone to take their seats. When he called for a moment of silence in memory of Howard and Marty, many in the crowd bowed their heads; some crossed themselves or muttered a prayer. Margaret stared straight ahead. Clarissa hunched forward, her gaze averted, her hair dangling in front of her face. Rachel leaned on Michael's shoulder with her eyes down.

Borges, of course, saw none of this. He sat motionless, one hand on his walking stick, his glassy eyes rolled toward the ceiling, as the moment of silence passed and Cliff introduced him to thunderous applause. Then he smiled a shy, astonished smile and silenced the crowd with a flick of the wrist. "My sincere thanks to Professor Jensen," he began in a tentative voice, "and to all of you, for your kind hospitality, and for coming here today"—his voice faltered, as if he couldn't remember what he intended to say—"to listen to a blind old man who may be able to cast some light on a difficult subject; a subject which may be perceived as tasteless under the circumstances, for which I apologize."

He smiled again and went on. "My topic today is 'On Murder Considered As One of the Fine Arts.' That, of course, is the title of an essay by Thomas De Quincey, published in 1827. I greatly admire De Quincey as a stylist, but I'm afraid his essay does not deliver what it promises. It does not tell us how to think about murder as one of the fine arts. If you were determined to commit a murder in the most artistic fashion possible, it would give you little guidance. And so today I'd like to speculate on what De Quincey might have said if he had stuck to his topic.

"You'll forgive me, I hope, if I use some literary illustrations. But let me be clear: Though my focus is aesthetic, I'm not speaking of murder as represented in literature or art. I mean the crime of murder itself. Such as—to take a recent instance—the murder of Professor Howard Vaughan."

A murmur ran through the room, but Borges ignored it. "First a few general principles. For a murder to be worthy of consideration as a work of art, it must be deliberate and premeditated, and the killer must be cold-blooded, calculating, and intent on evading punishment. A killer who aspires to the lofty status of artist must know that he is committing a heinous crime—he cannot act under color of law or authority—and he must use all the resources at his disposal to avoid detection and punishment. This will include ruthlessly casting suspicion on others. And even a murderer who meets these standards will be disqualified if he is a professional killer. For murder to be considered as one of the fine arts, it must be free of any commercial taint. With apologies to Raskolnikov, I would extend this prohibition to amateurs motivated by financial gain.

"This brings us to the question of motive. Murder may be committed for a variety of reasons, among them jealousy, spite, revenge, ambition, self-protection, the protection of others, a desire for justice and of course—probably the most common motive—financial gain. We have already dismissed financial gain. Jealousy, spite and revenge are also unworthy motives for an artist, as they are for a human being. So what are we left with? Self-protection, the protection of others, and the quest for justice. It is here that the aesthetic and moral universes intersect, as they inevitably must. I lay it down as axiomatic that *for a murder to be taken seriously as a work of art, it must be morally justified in the mind of the person who commits it.* Although the murderer cannot act under color of law, he must act under a claim of right."

Borges paused to allow his axiom to be appreciated. "Does anyone disagree?" Some people nodded, others grinned; no one spoke up. His manner was kindly but not so kindly as to invite disagreement, which, it was clear, he would not tolerate.

"Now," he said, "with these principles in mind, how does the murderer approach the task before him? The epitome of success is not to be caught and punished, but the murderer cannot attain this goal by making it appear that no crime has been committed. Artistically, that would be no success at all. It would be like a landscape painter pointing out the window instead of painting a picture. A work of art requires, at least potentially, some act of aesthetic contemplation by a person other than the artist. There must be an audience.

"In theory this may be an audience of one, consisting only of the victim. Poe's 'A Cask of Amontillado' comes to mind. But if the motive is justice, and not merely a private agenda of spite or revenge, then the crime should be visible beyond the killer and his victim. Justice is never a private affair. If justice is to be served, there must be others who become aware of the murder and the retribution it brings. And there must be at least one other person who learns about the crime, who sees the punishment that has been meted out and wonders what transgression could have justified it. That person is the detective.

"And so in this sense—this aesthetic sense that we are applying to the crime of murder—the detective is as necessary as the killer himself. He is responsible for the crime in the same way that a writer is responsible for his own precursors. How can this be? How can the detective be responsible for a crime that occurred *before* he'd ever heard of the killer or the victim? In destiny, events are connected like points on a sphere. The fallacy that time always runs in one direction—that Zeno's arrow must reach its target, that Achilles must eventually outrace the tortoise—has been refuted by thinkers too numerous to mention. And so the detective, when his ingenuity has been challenged, becomes responsible for the crime he is called upon to solve. It falls to him to close the circle of justice.

"This puts a great burden on the detective. For just as the murderer cannot be a professional, neither can the detective.   He certainly cannot be a policeman.   A policeman is like the guard in an art museum, who spends his days surrounded by masterpieces but has no appreciation for art, focusing on outward appearances with no awareness of the ideals of balance, order and symmetry that lie beneath the surface. No, when murder must be considered as one of the fine arts, the ideal detective is not a professional but a talented amateur.   He is (if I may say so) someone like me."

Borges stopped talking and faced the audience with his glassy stare for what seemed an eternity.   People started clapping, and a few stood up, thinking the lecture was over. Cliff rose and announced, "Let's take a fifteen minute break."

I led Borges off the dais to join his wife, who was entertaining the faculty with phrases from her Berlitz guide. Not to be outdone, the professors barraged Borges with stilted phrases of their own, which he brushed aside, interrogating them instead about their familiarity with H.P. Lovecraft and Miskatonic University.

"Miskatonic was actually... a fictitious university," Cliff explained.   "Lovecraft just made it up."

Borges glared skeptically in Cliff's direction.   "I doubt that very much."

Everyone laughed and Borges used that as an excuse to slip away.   He grasped my wrist and toddled toward the refreshment table, where some of the graduate students were debating the merits of what we later called postmodernism.   "Very clever idea," Michael Koch said, "that the detective is somehow responsible for the crime. But is it realistic? Or just a literary artifice?"

"Realistic," Borges said, "and therefore an artifice."

"I still prefer realism," Michael persisted.

"Do you prefer the realism of Cervantes, Henry James, or Franz Kafka?"

Before Michael could answer, he was elbowed aside by Clarissa Vaughan, who pressed in close to Borges and squeezed his hand. "Do you know who killed my father?" she asked in a low voice.

"I have some ideas," he smiled, leaning closer. "Perhaps you can help me. That story Marty Levin submitted for the anthology—you read it, didn't you?"

Her dark eyes narrowed. "Yeah, it sat on my Dad's desk for a long time."

"Did you write it?"

"Are you kidding? I could hardly stand to read it."

"Too brutal? Too unnerving?"

"Too stupid. It was like some surrealistic murder trial from a hundred years ago, with the lawyers wearing powdered wigs and all that. The defendant was a professor, the witnesses were everybody he'd ever abused—students, faculty, even his wife—and at the end the judge sentences him to be hanged."

Borges paused. "Did you ever talk to Marty about the story?"

"Sort of. When he called me."

"He called you? Was that after your father was killed?"

"Yeah. He asked me if I'd read the story. I said no but I guess he could tell I was lying." She blushed. "We were pretty good friends."

"What did he say?"

"He told me not to tell anyone. Even my mother."

"Your mother?"

"He said he didn't write the story and he had to talk to me. We were supposed to meet in the library but he never showed up. Then I found out he was dead."

"Did he kill himself?"

She shook her head. "Whoever killed my father killed Marty."

Borges reached out to touch her arm. "Just one more fact. When Marty called you, was that before or after your mother was arrested?"

"After. But she was out on bail by then."

A lean, balding man in a cheap brown suit touched my elbow. It was two in the afternoon and he was badly in need of a shave. "Excuse me," he said warily. "My name is Mike Petro. I need to have a word with Mr. Borges." He held up a badge that identified him as an Essex County police detective.

I pulled Borges aside and introduced him to Mr. Petro. They conferred in hushed tones for a few minutes before the man drifted away and took a seat in the back of the room. Borges seemed enchanted to have made the acquaintance of a real detective.

Back on the dais, he waited until absolute silence had been restored. "Now that we've established some general principles, I propose to apply them to an actual case: the recent murder of Professor Howard Vaughan. This may seem tasteless, but my personal honor is at stake." A note of indignation sharpened his voice. "I believe it was my topic for this seminar, and my syllabus, that led to Professor

Vaughan's death in the particular way it occurred. Naively, I chose De Quincey's essay and certain classic texts for what I thought would be an academic discussion. But in the killer's mind the crime had been conceived; malice aforethought lay curled up by the door like Cain's demon, waiting to be prodded into action. And the precise shape taken by the professor's murder—its conception and execution as a work of art—was inspired by my topic and my syllabus, for which I will never forgive myself."

He frowned with an expression that was at once remorseful and severe. "After learning of the crime, I issued a revised syllabus including the literary clues that baffled the police. Every one of those clues had been intended for me. The letters 'R-A-C-H-E'—taken straight from Conan Doyle's 'A Study in Scarlet'—were scrawled by the murderer, not by the victim. They told me that this was a crime to be judged by the aesthetic principles I planned to discuss at this seminar—and that I'd been chosen as the detective who must solve the crime.

"A blind detective? Is this a cruel joke? Perhaps; but my status was confirmed by the poem left open on Professor Vaughan's desk: T.S. Eliot's 'The Waste Land,' in which the most important personage is Tiresias, the blind soothsayer who revealed the crimes of Oedipus. He sees all, he foresuffers all; it is said that the gods gave him the gift of prophecy in compensation for his blindness. I have received no such compensation. And yet, unexpectedly, I find that I can see more clearly than others, past the accidents of everyday life to the Platonic forms that underlie them. I've accepted the role of detective with confidence. I'll never see the murderer's face, but I know something more important, something that goes beyond mere appearances: I know what books he has read."

Borges raised his palms in a pantomime of self-doubt. "Did I say 'he'? I must use a pronoun because I'm speaking English, not Spanish; I should have said 'he or she.' In fact a reading of 'The Waste Land' points strongly to a woman, Rachel O'Meara, as the prime suspect. Many years ago, when Rachel was a teenager in Sligo, Professor Vaughan caused her brother's death in a drunken accident. Later he returned to Ireland, where they had a love affair; he invited her here to complete her studies. When she arrived she first took up with a German graduate student named Michael Koch. Then about a month ago she renewed the affair with Professor Vaughan. Before long—but not before his wife had become insanely jealous—Professor Vaughan was found slumped over his desk with 'The Waste Land' opened to the very passage where Eliot quotes from *Tristan und Isolde*. Could anyone doubt that Rachel is Isolde, the wild Irish maid who consecrated her life to avenging her brother's death? She left her signature, and declared her purpose, in the ingenious quotation from Conan Doyle: the letters 'R-A-C-H-E,' which might be either the beginning of her name or the German word for revenge."

Half the audience twisted in their seats to stare at Rachel, the other half to avoid staring at her. She looked pale and desperate, mad with love and grief like the original Isolde. "Does that settle it, then?" Borges asked, his voice rising. "What about Michael Koch, the German student who must have hated Howard for taking Rachel away from him? Couldn't 'R-A-C-H-E' point to a German bent on revenge?"

Now all eyes—including Rachel's—were on Michael, who turned away with a bitter smile. "And there's another suspect," Borges pressed on, "though again it may seem tasteless to name him: Marty Levin. He submitted a story for Professor Vaughan's anthology and then tried to withdraw it. The professor refused, and on his desk lay the story of Cardillac, who killed in order to retrieve his artistic creations. Marty, like Cardillac, could not bear to part with his work—did he take drastic steps to get it back?" Clarissa squinted at Borges with a crazed expression, as if she'd taken his metaphors literally and blamed him for her father's death, and possibly for Marty's.

"So that's all we have—'The Waste Land,' 'A Study in Scarlet,' *Tristan und Isolde*, 'Mademoiselle de Scudéry'—a jumble of literary evidence that incriminates an assortment of people who all had their reasons for killing Howard Vaughan."

Borges thumped his walking stick on the floor. "I could not ignore the challenge implied by these clues which had been planted solely for my benefit, daring me, defying me, to solve the crime." He waved an accusing finger toward the crowd and addressed the murderer: "I know you, *hypocrite lecteur!* You are cold-blooded, calculating, and intent on evading punishment by casting suspicion on others! You are an artist!"

He leaned forward, gathering the entire room into his oracular gaze. "You recorded your fantasy of killing Howard Vaughan in the missing manuscript—yes, you wrote the story submitted by Marty Levin—and yet it was still just a fantasy, awaiting inspiration to transform it into art. When Rachel O'Meara arrived from Ireland, still mourning her dead brother, and fell in love with the man who'd been sent to bring her from the airport, the resemblance to the legend of Tristan and Isolde was almost too powerful to resist. And then when Rachel resumed her affair with Professor Vaughan and the topic of this seminar was announced, you saw the opportunity of a lifetime: the chance to commit a murder worthy of consideration among the fine arts, a murder as aesthetically satisfying as it was brutal and vindictive. You had read all the books on the syllabus, and many more. There would never be another moment like this, never a moment when so many archetypes—or so many suspects—could be called into action.

"With small effort you could plant enough evidence to implicate Rachel O'Meara and Michael Koch if anyone with sufficient discernment cared to investigate (and you knew I would be the detective). The manuscript could disappear as long as an alternative explanation surfaced—the tale of Cardillac—to incriminate Marty Levin and explain why he needed to retrieve it. Marty knew who wrote that story, so he knew who the killer was. Perhaps he confronted you; perhaps you hunted him down. In either case, he had to die."

Borges settled back in his chair and reverted to his benign, self-deprecating smile. "False clues point to false conclusions," he said, "directing us away from the real killer to other suspects. You made a classic mistake—you planted a clue against every suspect *except yourself*. That's how I knew where to look: at the person against whom there was no evidence. At the dog that didn't bark."

He chuckled at his own joke and went on: "Perhaps I should put it differently: we should look at the person against whom there is no *credible* evidence. Ludicrous, obviously planted evidence, such as clues out of Conan

Doyle, may serve to distract us from a person's actual guilt. For example, Margaret Vaughan has done an excellent job of deflecting attention to Marty Levin, who died just after she was released from jail. And what of the daughter, Clarissa? Either one of them could have written that story and asked Marty to submit it for the purpose of torturing Professor Vaughan. And there's no evidence whatever against Clarissa."

Clarissa and Margaret glared back at Borges with murder in their eyes. "As always we must return to the question of motive," he went on heedlessly. "There's something missing from the clues you left at the scene of the crime. You left 'The Waste Land' but not *Macbeth*; *Tristan und Isolde* but not *Richard III* or *Othello*. The motive that's missing is the one that accounts for the murder of Howard Vaughan—*ambition*. Or perhaps I should say, thwarted ambition distorted by spite. But there's more to it than that. For a murder to be taken seriously as a work of art, as we have seen, the murderer must regard himself as an instrument of justice. If he does not—if his motive, like Macbeth's, is blind ambition—he will trip over the demon lurking by the door and find himself groping in the darkness to wipe the blood from his hands. Even Iago thought he had justice on his side.

"And so when I look for the murderer of Howard Vaughan, I look for a man—yes, it is a man—consumed by ambition, nursing decades of grievances and convinced that he is an instrument of justice. He has read all the books— too many books, as it seems. He is judged superior by his peers. He should have been the chairman of the department. Yet instead he's lived the life of a lackey, scorned, laughed at, humiliated on a daily basis by Howard Vaughan."

Beside me on the dais I could hear rustling papers, labored breathing, the scooting of a chair leg. As I turned I saw Cliff Jensen lurch to his feet, clutching his papers as he hurried out the door. His footsteps receded down the hall.

The room echoed with a mortuary silence. "What I just heard," Borges said, "and you just witnessed, was Professor Jensen's confession."

There were a few gasps, some whispering, some muted objections, before the silence settled again. Detective Petro eased out of his seat and slipped through the door. Borges sat motionless, like a conductor waiting to raise his baton.

"Please go on," Rachel moaned.

"Mr. Jensen is undoubtedly the murderer, as I'm sure the police will be able to confirm. At this moment, alerted by the detective who just left the auditorium, they are waiting at his home with a search warrant. Without much effort they will find the missing manuscript, with its fantasy of Howard Vaughan's trial and execution, written by Mr. Jensen and submitted, as a prank, by the unfortunate Marty Levin, who trusted his advisor and would have done anything for him. It's obviously based on the legal proceedings against Professor Vaughan in Ireland, with its lawyers in powdered wigs—Mr. Jensen was there and the imagery must have stuck in his mind; he even told me that Professor Vaughan could have been hanged, which I'm sure was an exaggeration. Since Mr. Jensen is proud of his work as a murderer and believes it was morally justified, he will confess and avoid the necessity of a trial."

"But why?" Margaret cried out. "Why would Cliff want to kill Howard?"

"The motive will not be hard to establish," Borges smiled. "With all due respect, Professor Vaughan seems to have been hated by everyone who knew him. He was an exploitative, untrustworthy, mean-spirited drunk. There's probably no one here who never experienced the occasional desire to do him in."

Margaret burst into tears and had to be escorted from the room by Clarissa. Rachel and Michael and the others sat frozen in their seats, anxious to learn how they would fare in the judgment the old soothsayer was rendering. I felt a twinge of guilt when I remembered how much I'd hated Howard. Had I ever actually wished him dead?

"I suspected Mr. Jensen from the beginning," Borges went on, "on literary grounds, as I have explained. But I understood that such evidence is not enough to support a search warrant, let alone a conviction; and so I turned my attention to the missing manuscript. The killer had to be the one who wrote that story, but that could have been Marty or Margaret or Clarissa or even the young man sitting beside me"—he meant me—"and it wasn't until today, when Clarissa described the actual content of the story, that I could positively identify it as having been written by Mr. Jensen.

"I acknowledge my own complicity. My seminar topic floated the idea of murder as one of the fine arts; my syllabus lighted the path from motive to action; and my availability as the detective proved too great a temptation. Yet the actual killing of Howard Vaughan—which now seems pre-ordained, like Zeno's arrow finally hitting its target—could only have been carried out by Professor Jensen. It was his destiny to commit that crime."

Everyone in the room breathed an inner sigh of relief: the murder was Jensen's doing, not ours. But Borges would not let us off so easily. "We must all certainly deplore what Professor Jensen did. Yet we should bear in mind that the difference between Mr. Jensen and ourselves—and I mean every man and woman in this room, excluding, of course, my wife—is more a difference of literary genealogy than moral culpability."

He cast his kindly, imperious gaze over the crowd— like many gifted speakers, he had the knack of appearing to speak directly to each member of the audience—and then rolled his sightless eyes toward me. "If you had read the same books as Professor Jensen, in the same order, you would probably be as guilty as he is. And it might very well be you who just ran fleeing from the room."

∞

I'm an old man now, older than Borges was when I knew him. Like all old men, I nurse the illusion that if I can remember enough of the past and imagine enough of the future, I will never reach the end of my life, or if I do, it will take forever to get there. Right now I'm sitting at my kitchen table, ignoring the putrid smell wafting up from under the sink as I wait for one of my daughters to call and wish me a happy birthday. I wonder which daughter it will be? Ingrid is the older of the two, the handmaiden of conscience, justice and regret. She inhabits the past, as it was or should have been; she tends her mother's grave and invests in mine. Gracie is three years younger, the personification of action and imagination. She inhabits the present and all possible futures: she still thinks she'll marry a prince. I love both of them, of course, beyond anything else.

Gracie spends most of her time at the gym or hanging around in bars with her friends, while Ingrid works sixty hours a week as a tax attorney. And yet it's Ingrid who calls to say happy birthday.

"Has Gracie called?" she asks me.

"Not yet."

"Did you even remember it was your birthday?"

"Of course I remembered," I reassure her. "There's nothing wrong with my memory."

"Not wrong, exactly. Just different."

"For example, I can remember what you were wearing on Christmas—dark blue pants, a red blouse and turquoise earrings—and what you served for breakfast: an omelet made with cheddar cheese, bacon and jalapeño peppers."

"You didn't like it much."

"It was delicious, as I mentioned at the time."

"There are two ways your memory can go," she says, laughing. "You can stop remembering things that happened, or start remembering things that didn't."

Most old men lose their memories; I've lost my imagination. Sweet memory is my only muse. She visits at odd times, always unexpectedly, staying a few seconds or a few hours according to her whim. She distracts me from my reading, interrupts as I listen to music, whispers tales in my ear when I try to fall asleep. Sometimes one thing leads to another and she stays the night, stirring my loneliness with some forgotten passion. With the approach of dawn she falls silent and fades away. But she always leaves me a little souvenir, a story I can add to my collection if I write it down soon enough. Ingrid—who has never had an imagination—thinks I'm making it all up. She doesn't think I ever met Borges, or, if I did, that we ever solved a crime together or prowled Cambridge in a Ford Galaxie or shared a booth at a coffee shop in Somerville. If I met him, she says, it was probably at some reception in his honor, where I sidled up and mumbled a few words—"Señor Borges, my name is Nick Martin"—and slipped away before he could answer. Admittedly that sounds like the sort of thing I would have done, and sometimes did, so I can't rule it out;

but I believe that with Borges things were destined to happen quite differently, almost magically, as in a dream. Because of him I met the love of my life, and everything else, sad as it may seem now, has followed from that. To give Ingrid her due, there may be more than meets the eye in these stories, some secret that won't be revealed until I remember the last one. A secret to be revealed, not within the dream, but when the dreamer awakes.

Memory has lost her sweetness since the accident. Now most often she appears in the robes of her ugly stepsister, regret; the perfect complement to the back pain that torments me day and night. My daughters seldom see eye to eye, but since their mother left us they are in agreement about one thing: me. I have become a problem. By today's standards I'm not very old, but in their opinion I'm too debilitated to stay here alone in the apartment where I've lived for twenty-five years. And now there's a leaky pipe under the sink. It puts out a nasty smell, but I try to look on the bright side. As long as the odor of putrefaction and death is seeping in through a pipe under the sink, it's not coming from me.

Ingrid and Gracie use every ounce of their energy to try to persuade me to move into assisted living, which sounds a little too much like assisted suicide for my taste. The last time they were here they homed in on that smell like a couple of frenzied coon hounds. "What's that awful smell? Where's it coming from?"

"Just a leak under the sink," I said. "Don't worry, I'm going to fix it."

Ingrid looked as if she was about to be sick. "No way you're going to fix it. Have you called the landlord?"

"Not yet," I admitted. "Katie—your mother—always paid the rent. I don't even know who the landlord is."

"That does it. You've got to get out of this place."

Ingrid opened the door under the sink and peeked inside. "Raw sewage!" She backed away in disgust and slammed the door. "I'm sure it's a code violation. It'll make you sick. After you get out of here, we'll sue the landlord."

"I'm not going to move," I said calmly, "and I'm not going to sue the landlord."

"Why not?"

"I guess I feel some kind of loyalty after all this time."

"Loyalty? To a landlord who lets you suffer?"

"Who *wants* you to suffer?" Gracie frowned.

They're right. It doesn't make much sense. Maybe I just don't want to move. Yes, this apartment is a dump, but would the next one be any better? None of the other tenants know any more about the landlord than I do, though some of them claim to have seen him in the building. Mr. Tartini, who has lived down the hall since the beginning of time, says the place was much better maintained in the old days. The landlord—Mr. Tartini can't remember his name—used to come down himself and repair the plumbing and keep the boiler working properly. He cared about the tenants and wanted them to be happy. "Now you never see him anymore," Mr. Tartini says. "Maybe he's dead, or retired to Florida. You send in your rent, but try getting anything done."

I promised Ingrid and Gracie that I'd look into getting the pipe fixed, but even with the smell as a constant reminder, I doubt if I'll give it a very high priority. I've got memories to deal with.

It would be too much to say that Borges had been humbled by the way the Vaughan case played out—that would have required something on the order of the Big Bang. But his maiden voyage as a detective had left him deeply troubled. Though he'd brought a killer to justice, he'd been forced to acknowledge his own complicity in Cliff Jensen's crime. It was the failure of literature that troubled him the most. Art, he'd told me once, is always about justice and morality. But what value does it have if it doesn't make you a better person? How could Cliff read all those books and still do what he did? And what about the rest of us? Is a spectator really no better than an accomplice? If I'd read the same books as Cliff, in the same order, would I be any less guilty than he was?

Such were the questions—though neither of us gave voice to them—that rumbled beneath the surface as Borges and I drove back to Cambridge. Our adventure was over but we decided to keep meeting for breakfast whenever we could—a decision that would lead to further ordeals of crime and punishment in which our images of ourselves and each other, of man and the universe, of reality and its alternatives, would be put to the test. Those questions, and quite a few others, would bubble to the surface now and then, momentarily finding answers or dissolving, as most such questions do, into the river of memory and imagination that we call life.

Borges never tired of talking about Chuang Tzu and his famous dream. The ancient Chinese sage fell asleep and dreamed he was a butterfly; and when he awoke, he wondered if he was Chuang Tzu dreaming of a butterfly or a butterfly dreaming he was Chuang Tzu. To Borges this story stood for the insubstantiality of time and human personality. To me it suggests something different, which may be the same thing: that the dream and the dreamer are one. Chuang Tzu is the butterfly, and the butterfly is Chuang Tzu.

Memory and imagination are the mind's mirrors, one an image of the past, the other of a future that never comes. When the mirrors are turned to face each other, they project a mystery too vast for the mind that contains them. Many a mind has unraveled there, or split in half; some have seen ghosts. Now that my birthday is past, I've been thinking about the next case I worked on with Borges, which I've described in a tale called "The Madman in the Library." It's the story of a man who lost his mind in the attempt to find it and his life in the attempt to live it—and whose greatest fear was a ghost he didn't believe in.

2.

The Madman in the Library

PHILOSOPHY, *n.*   A route of many roads leading from nowhere to nothing.

> Ambrose Bierce, *The Devil's Dictionary.*

My career as a graduate student in Comparative Literature at Ipswich University was off to a rocky start, with the arrest of my faculty advisor for the murder of our department head. Many in the department blamed me, not for the murder but for its detection. Cliff Jensen was very well liked, and it didn't help my case that Comparative Literature itself had supplied the clues that led to his arrest, since I had provided assistance to the only man in the world who knew the subject well enough to solve the crime: Jorge Luis Borges. But was that fair, really? All I'd done was drive the aging poet around the New England countryside, read to him, and act as his interpreter when it served his purposes not to understand English. I'd made my small contribution, as had Thomas De Quincey and a local police detective named Mike Petro, but it was Borges who'd unmasked Cliff Jensen as the killer.

The Boston papers, particularly the *Globe*, played up the case and touted Borges's success as a detective (which, he confessed privately, gave him more pleasure than all the honors he'd earned as a writer). Yet Borges refused to be interviewed or photographed in relation to the case; he always shunned the limelight if it interfered with what he wanted to do. He showed scant interest in his duties at Harvard and rarely set foot on the campus, preferring to spend his mornings with me in our coffee shop in Somerville. There, on a typical morning, he sat sipping maté and nibbling cheese danishes while I absorbed potfuls of black coffee and kept my eye on the dark-haired waitress who, I liked to think, also gazed occasionally in my direction. "I think I'm in love with the waitress," I told Borges.

"Of course," he said. "Do you know her name?"

I did not.

"Then I will call her Diotima," he said, "after the female sage who taught Socrates everything he knew about love. Let's hope she has something to teach you."

One morning, after Diotima had brought our breakfast and I'd settled down with my *Record-American*, hoping to catch up on the hockey scores, Borges brought up De Quincey's essay, "On Murder Considered As One Of The Fine Arts," which had played such a decisive role in the unmasking of Cliff Jensen as the murderer of Howard Vaughan. "One of the striking things about that essay," Borges said, "is De Quincey's dictum that all philosophers, sooner or later, are murdered."

"Except Hobbes," I reminded him.

"Quite right," he chuckled, echoing De Quincey's amazement that Thomas Hobbes, of all people, had not been murdered. "But all the others—Descartes and

Spinoza, for example—were either murdered or suffered attempts on their life."

"According to De Quincey." I didn't want to contradict Borges (that was never a good idea) but I'd done a little research and found no support for De Quincey's bizarre theory. "I wonder—"

"Now the only question," Borges interrupted, "is Why? Why is it that philosophers, seemingly the most harmless of men—since few pay attention to their theories, and even fewer put them into practice—should so often be the subject of homicide?"

"That's a very good question, assuming—"

"Take Spinoza, for example. Surely the most benign, most admirable man of his day. Yet De Quincey says he was murdered."

"Probably just an apocryphal anecdote."

"All anecdotes are apocryphal," Borges smiled. "De Quincey said that too, and I agree with him."

Borges's clouded but imperious gaze told me, as if I didn't already know, that nothing could be gained by questioning the dogma that all philosophers are murdered. The only question, as he said, was Why? "All right, then," I said. "Why?"

"I am a poet," he declared, surprisingly. "If I were ever murdered, I hope it would be on account of my poetry. Not by some pickpocket or some madman or some jilted lover settling a personal score."

I thought I knew where he was going. "Then if you were a philosopher...."

"I'd want to be murdered on account of my philosophy. On account of my ideas."

"Ideas can be dangerous."

He nodded emphatically. "Take Descartes, for example. He was almost murdered by cut-throat sailors on a voyage in the North Sea when he was twenty-five years old. De Quincey assumes that the motive was robbery, but perhaps a more fitting motive would have been Descartes's theory of dualism."

"Dualism?"

Suddenly I became aware of Diotima standing beside our booth, smiling wanly as if, in the annals of waitresshood, this conversation set a new low. Now she could say she'd heard it all.

"Yes, dualism," Borges went on, oblivious to her presence. "The idea that the body and the mind, the physical and the spiritual, are absolutely and utterly distinct, separated by an unbridgeable gulf that's woven into the fabric of the cosmos. And that the human mind—which according to Descartes is all we can really know—is trapped inside the body like a fly in a bottle."

"Can I get you anything else?" Diotima ventured.

"No, thanks," I told her. "Not right now."

Borges wanted only to finish his thought. "The ghost in the machine, it's been called. We're only now beginning to recover from Descartes's monstrous invention."

Diotima winked at me and strolled away.

"But what's the alternative?" I asked Borges.

"Monism, obviously. One-ism, if you will. The belief that mind and body are different attributes of the same big Something—whether that be God, Nature, Brahman, the Tao. Whatever it is, it's all there is, and everything else is just a manifestation of it. That was Spinoza's philosophy, and he was murdered for it."

"According to De Quincey."

Borges waved my comment aside as a vexatious impertinence. "The question is: Would history have been different if things had gone the other way? What if Descartes had been murdered and Spinoza spared? If those cut-throats had been successful, would we now live in a world of pantheistic monism instead of the Cartesian dualism which has led to most of our problems for the past three hundred years?"

"I don't know, I assume—"

"And do you suppose it was just a coincidence that Spinoza was actually murdered instead of Descartes? A simple twist of fate? Or was there something deeper going on? Something darker, more sinister, more conducive"—he waved his hand ambiguously—"to certain forces working behind the scenes?"

I couldn't help laughing. "You mean some sort of conspiracy to foist dualism on the world?"

Borges smiled his most disingenuous smile. "Only a madman could believe that."

The next morning we were surprised to find Mike Petro, the Essex County police detective who'd helped Borges snag Cliff Jensen, waiting for us at the coffee shop. Petro was a classic detective—taciturn, wary, and in need of a shave at ten in the morning. For all I knew he had a sentimental streak, maybe a soft spot for children and pets, though all I'd seen so far was the humorless professionalism of a man who'd spent his career excavating in the ruins of human lives. Borges couldn't have been more excited to find him there. He sat him down in our booth, called for maté and coffee, and peppered him with questions about cases he'd solved, detectives he'd known, criminals he'd sent to jail. Petro seemed nervous, distracted, scarcely able to pay attention to Borges's questions, let alone answer them. He twirled his hat in his hands and set it on the table. He fished in the pockets of his reversible raincoat until he found his cigarettes, then slipped them into his shirt pocket without taking one out. His restless eye seemed to be plotting an escape route through the kitchen.

Suddenly he cut Borges off and blurted out the reason for his visit. "It's about my nephew," he said, keeping his voice low. "My sister's boy. He's been arrested."

"Is he in jail?" Borges asked.

"No, worse than that. They've got him in Danvers."

The mention of Danvers State Hospital (formerly known as the Danvers State Lunatic Asylum) sent a little chill down my spine. I'd glimpsed the institution from a distance as I explored the back roads south of Ipswich. Built in the 1870s, it was a congeries of dark Neo-Gothic structures topped with a mad forest of gables, towers and turrets and linked together (if local folklore could be believed) by a hidden network of underground passages. In recent years the hospital had endured a barrage of negative publicity—reports of patient beatings, suicides, and the indiscriminate use of strait jackets, lobotomies and shock therapy—and pressure to close it was mounting. I was amazed to hear they were still sending people there.

"How old is your nephew?" I asked Mike.

"He'll be twenty next month."

The thought of a young life being wasted and tortured in such a place made me queasy, even though—or perhaps because—I was only a few years older.

"Is he insane?" Borges asked.

"They're saying paranoid schizophrenia, but frankly I don't believe it. I've known Ted all his life. A couple years ago he got mixed up with the wrong crowd. Started taking drugs and letting his hair grow long. His Dad, my sister's husband Pete—let me just put it this way: he's an opinionated, hot-tempered guy and he didn't like it. They had a big fight and Ted ran off and joined a hippie commune. Pete calls it a cult. Now he got picked up on a drug charge and they put him in Danvers, which is the last place he ought to be."

Borges hesitated, undoubtedly wondering (as I was) what Mike expected him to do about all this. "Has your nephew—Ted is his name?—seemed normal up to now?"

"He's always been a dreamer," Mike said. "A little detached from reality. When the other kids were out playing ball, he'd stay inside reading books."

Borges grimaced. "Someone who reads books is detached from reality?"

"I didn't mean it that way." Mike tried to placate Borges with a string of disclaimers, but I knew he wouldn't succeed. The image of a pathetic little boy staying inside reading books while the other kids played outside struck a little too close to home. Borges's grimace resolved into a frown.

"My sister wants to meet you and I was hoping she could tell you about this herself," Mike went on. "The thing is, most of the books Ted reads are about philosophy. You know, Plato and Aristotle and that type of thing. He wants to be a philosopher when he grows up, if he ever grows up. He told me he considers himself a philosopher already."

"This is very grave indeed," Borges intoned, teasing him.

"I promised my sister I'd talk to you about it."

"I'm not sure why."

Mike's eyes flitted around the room, making sure that no one was listening. "He thinks somebody's trying to kill him."

"If he's a philosopher," Borges said, suppressing a smile, "somebody probably is."

Mike's sister Evelyn lived in the gritty North Shore town of Lynn, half an hour northeast of Cambridge, in a low, ramshackle house patched together with gray weathered siding. She was as nervous and grim as her brother, though not as badly in need of a shave. Her husband, a burly Greek immigrant named Pete Rodis, looked almost old enough to be Ted's grandfather. His family (we'd learned from Mike) had suffered grievously under the Nazis and then under the Communists. He emigrated to America, where he married Evelyn and went into the floor-covering business. Ted was their only child.

Mrs. Rodis led us down a short but richly carpeted hallway to a small sitting room dominated by a television set, where she seated us on a low couch facing a coffee table, piled high with newspapers and magazines, that seemed to creep up and bang our shins when we sat down. The husband, who didn't look happy to see us, occupied the only other comfortable chair—a brown Naugahyde Barcalounger—leaving Mrs. Rodis to drag a metal chair in from the kitchen. For a few minutes we talked about the route we'd driven from Cambridge and whether the house had been hard to find. Then we talked about how much we enjoyed working with Mike and the critical role he'd played in the Jensen case. Inevitably the conversation gravitated to the purpose of our visit and a topic the couple was in the habit of avoiding—their son Ted.

"He's a good boy," Mrs. Rodis said. "Just a little more sensitive than most."

"He's always been nuts," Mr. Rodis growled.

"When the other kids were out riding their bikes, he'd stay inside reading philosophy books."

The old man beamed triumphantly. "I rest my case!"

"The problems only started after he got involved with drugs."

Mr. Rodis leaned forward and appealed to Borges with a sweeping gesture, as if he hadn't noticed that his visitor was blind. "Then he got really out of touch with reality. Started listening to that hippie music, growing his hair long, playing the guitar—"

"And then when he joined that cult," his wife cut in, "that Mel Lyman cult—"

"A bunch of hippies worshipping a lunatic who thinks he's God!"

The mother's face darkened. "If you didn't drive him out of the house he would have been OK. He would never have heard of Mel Lyman, but oh, no, you had to give him one of your famous ultimatums."

The old man threw up his hands and laughed. "Listen to her! The kid was so zonked out on drugs he was asking me, how do I know anything really exists? How do I know the world is still here when I close my eyes?"

"He's a creative thinker," she pleaded. "He asks questions nobody else is asking."

"He's a goddamn atheist, that's what he is! How do I know anything exists?" Ted's father raised his fist. "I'll tell you how—"

Mrs. Rodis held up her hands as if she expected her husband to punch her. "He's a pantheist. That's what he told me."

"What the hell is a pantheist?" he yelled.

"Pantheism is the belief that God and the Universe are one."

Mr. Rodis smashed his fist down on the coffee table, knocking a pile of magazines onto the floor. "God and the Universe are not one!"

"So you know everything? You've seen God and the Universe and you know exactly what they are?"

"It's blasphemy to say they're the same thing!" The old man was on his feet, circling the coffee table like a caged animal. "If that's true, then every crime, every monstrosity, every act of evil, is part of God. Evil itself is part of God. Hitler and Stalin are part of God!"

His wife bowed her head, apparently defeated by this argument, but Borges came to her rescue: "An Irish philosopher once speculated that at the end of time all things, even evil, even the devil himself, will be absorbed back into God."

Mr. Rodis's face was purple. "You can tell your Irish philosopher for me: Hitler and Stalin will never be part of God, even at the end of time! I lost my family thanks to those monsters. Nobody's allowed to say that in my house!" He stared down at his shaking hands and stomped out of the room.

I handed Borges his ivory-handled walking stick and stood up. "I think we'd better be going."

"I apologize for my husband's outbursts," Mrs. Rodis murmured. "That's the way he is. I'm sorry. He's very upset about Ted."

"I understand," Borges said.

"We're both beside ourselves, trying to understand what's going on, trying to figure out what we should do."

Borges touched her hand. "I'm not a physician," he said. "But I think I know what ails your son: Metaphysical idealism."

"Is that a disease?"

"No, it's a philosophy. It's the belief that the material world we see, hear and touch doesn't exist as such. All that exists are minds and their ideas and perceptions."

"Then the world's just an illusion?" she smiled, as if the idea appealed to her.

"Not necessarily. Another Irish philosopher, Bishop Berkeley, argued that the world, when we're not perceiving or thinking about it, still exists in the mind of God."

Mr. Rodis burst back in and kicked another pile of magazines off the coffee table. "You and your philosophers can all go to hell, as far as I'm concerned! Get out of here!"

Borges was unruffled by the theatrics. I helped him to his feet and guided him slowly toward the door. "One last question," he said to Mrs. Rodis. "Does your son have any enemies?"

"No, of course not," she said. "Why would he have enemies?"

Her husband shouted out his own answer. "He sure thinks he does. The government, the FBI, the dualists—"

Borges's step faltered. "The dualists?"

"Don't ask me who they are," the old man said. "Ask his doctor. He thinks they're trying to kill him."

Borges seemed lost in thought as we edged our way out to my aging Ford Galaxie. As usual, he sat in the back seat and propped himself up with his walking stick.

"I think Philip Larkin wrote a poem about that pair," I said as we drove out of town. Borges remained silent, his sightless eyes seemingly fixed on the passing landscape.

"The poor kid's been caught in the middle of this his whole life," I added, hoping to elicit some response. "No wonder he's insane."

"If he's insane," Borges said, "it has nothing to do with his parents. They obviously have no influence on him."

"You think it's the drugs, then?"

Borges made a derisive noise and tapped his walking stick on the floor. "All my life," he said, "I've maintained a belief in metaphysical idealism. Even today I suspect that it's correct, preferable to materialism—and certainly to dualism, which tries to strike an impossible compromise between the two. But like infinity, which is undoubtedly real, idealism can't be grasped by the human mind. The man who attempts to follow it to its logical conclusion will be lost in a labyrinth of contradictions and must certainly go mad."

"But in Ted's case," I argued, "it's more than just metaphysical confusion. He thinks everybody's out to kill him."

"There's enormous pressure to escape into dualism. It may be a false picture of reality, but it suits the world's purposes quite well"—he'd started thumping the floor with a steady, mechanical beat, like the tread of an army of zealots—"and if you resist, the vast conspiracy of everyday life will press you into obedience with the tenacity of the Spanish Inquisition."

"So you think maybe this pressure—"

He cut me off with a climactic thump, loud enough
that for an instant I thought my muffler had fallen off.
"That's why the dualists—whoever they are—have been
tormenting poor Ted Rodis. It's not enough to lock him
up. They want him dead."

That night a winter storm paid a surprise visit, staying just
long enough to cushion our world with a soft and
deceptively attractive blanket of snow. I awoke with a
headache and the beginnings of a bad cold. Gazing out my
window, I saw beauty, the wonder of nature, and a chance
to spend the rest of the day in bed. The weather report
confirmed the wisdom of this aspiration. Beneath the
lovely snowscape—refuting the assumption that perception
and reality are one—lay an insidious layer of ice that was
wreaking havoc on the roads and highways of the
Commonwealth. Not the sort of morning to venture out in
the Galaxie, I concluded. But then the phone rang: it was
Borges, and he viewed the storm as a piece of effrontery.
He'd made up his mind to meet Ted Rodis that morning
and nothing could stop him. Indeed, he'd already called the
hospital and made an appointment with its director, Dr.
Jonathan Corwin.

I picked Borges up at his apartment in Cambridge. His
wife mumbled elegant phrases from her Berlitz guide as I
gathered his hat and cane and ushered him out the door.
We drove slowly up through Medford and Reading and
then traced a back route to the ancient hospital, winding our
way along icy roads overhung with the bowed tops of
evergreens and the gnarled branches of maples and oaks.

The car labored up a long hill and the hospital loomed over us, sinister and enormous, its gables and turrets shrouded in mist and smoke. My headache pounded unbearably.

"Something you may or may not know about Danvers," Borges said, "is that in the late seventeenth century—at the time of the infamous Salem witch trials—it was known as Salem Village."

"No," I disagreed. "Salem's a different place. It's a little south of here."

"What you call Salem was then known as Salem Town. Salem Village, which is where the witch craze began, is now called Danvers. And this hospital was built on Hathorne Hill, named after the judge who sent the largest number of witches to the gallows."

I eased the Galaxie down the unplowed driveway and parked as near as I could to the hospital's entrance. By the time I'd extricated Borges from the car and led him across the icy parking lot, I felt light-headed, almost faint. We were met at the door by a hefty middle-aged nurse, identified on her name tag as Mrs. Edith White, R.N. She was all smiles, in stark contrast to the pair of white-jacketed thugs lurking behind her, whose distracted stares made them look more like inmates than orderlies. "Can I help you?" she asked.

"Good morning, madam," Borges said with a chivalrous bow. "I am Jorge Luis Borges, formerly Director of the National Library of Argentina."

She smiled sweetly. "Come right in, sir!"

Mrs. White winked at me as I squeezed past her into the lobby. "We've had kings, presidents, Indian chiefs, visitors from outer space," she whispered. "This will be our first librarian."

The orderlies locked their arms around Borges's elbows and started to lead him away. "Wait a minute!" I protested. "He's not here as a patient."

The nurse eyed me skeptically. "And who are you?"

I gave her my name, and she seemed surprised that it wasn't Napoleon or Jesus Christ. "He's here to see the director," I told her. "Dr. Corwin. They spoke on the phone this morning."

One of the orderlies lurched toward me, wrapping an enormous hand around my wrist. He glared at me through his peculiar, fishlike eyes with what I can only describe as loathing. I later learned that his name was Floyd Akers and he'd been born in the hospital to a schizophrenic mother who was raped by one of the security guards.

"One moment, please," Mrs. White said, picking up a desk phone.

"It's about Ted Rodis," I explained.

That clarification seemed to send Floyd Akers over the brink. The very mention of Ted Rodis made him clench his teeth and snuffle like a mad dog. He tightened his grip on my wrist and clamped his free hand over my shoulder as if he intended to break my neck.

"That's enough, Floyd! Let him go!" Mrs. White said, and then she smiled at me. "Don't mind Floyd. He and Ted don't see eye to eye." That I could understand. The only way you could see eye to eye with Floyd Akers would be if your eyes were six inches apart.

Dr. Corwin was a spindly man of about sixty with a British accent and a kindly smile. "Dr. Corwin," I said, shaking his hand. "Very pleased to meet you. Allow me to introduce"— I took a wild gamble, desperate to keep

Borges from identifying himself again as a librarian—"Dr. Borges, of Buenos Aires."

"Dr. Borges," the Director repeated, bowing respectfully.

Borges, of course, ignored this gesture, which added to his authority. He cut an impressive figure in his dark suit and overcoat—tall, slightly stooped, his gray hair wispy and ethereal, his upturned, empty eyes letting it be known that they would not be deceived by mere appearances. "I've been engaged as a consultant, you understand," he said, "with respect to the Rodis boy."

"Of course, Dr. Borges."

Dr. Corwin led us into his office and sat us in front of his cluttered desk. I soon realized that he spoke mostly in sentence fragments. "Brought in by the police, unfortunately," he said. "Rather limits what we can do with him. Fine young man, in spite of it all—can't help but like him. Classic paranoid schizophrenic, but a most unusual view of the world—convinced it doesn't exist. Idealism, he calls it. Still, he's afraid of everything that moves. Thinks everybody's out to kill him—the orderlies, the security guards, the FBI. Of course Mel Lyman and the members of his commune."

"Mel Lyman?"

"Hippie guru runs a commune in Boston. Claims to be an incarnate god—puts out a paper called *Avatar*—followers seem to believe it. Including Ted, I suppose—ran off and joined them after an argument with his father. Oh, did I mention Ted's father? He's trying to kill him too."

"May I speak with the patient?" Borges asked.

"Certainly. He's working in the library this morning."

Dr. Corwin opened a door behind his desk and led us down a dimly-lighted corridor that smelled like the inside of a tomb. My throat tightened as I breathed the musty air, and the legend of Danvers State Hospital took hold of my imagination: the dark gables and turrets, the rumors of lobotomies and shock treatments, the underground passageways closed in by slimy, narrowing walls—and if Borges could be believed, the legacy of the Salem witch trials.

Borges's familiar voice brought me back to my senses. "This hospital," he said as we emerged into a wider but still shadowy hall, "was the model for Lovecraft's Arkham Sanitarium."

Dr. Corwin didn't catch the reference, but Borges's comment put him on the defensive. "Model for many fine institutions," he said. "We've had our problems, I won't try to deny it. Suicides and such—but what do you expect? All very troubled or they wouldn't be here, would they? And now the men in the green eye-shades want to shut it down."

"You mean the government? They're cutting the budget?"

"A great many troubled people," the doctor nodded. "Only home they've ever known. Give 'em more drugs, they say. Send 'em back to the community. Costs too much to keep 'em here."

A door opened at the far end of the hall and an elderly clergyman shuffled toward us, clutching a book in his gnarled hands. His suit was shabby, but when he smiled he emanated a timeless spiritual glow. "Are you here to see Ted Rodis?" he asked. "I'm Reverend Pendragon. I just spoke with Ted this morning. He's a good boy, a fine boy—but very mixed up, I'm afraid. Seems to doubt his own existence."

"Is he right or wrong about that?" Borges asked mischievously.

The clergyman's lips quivered as he struggled with the question. "We... all have our doubts," he stammered, "but given proper guidance...."

"There's hope, then?"

"The Lord takes care of his own." A flash of defiance lighted his eyes. "I must be going. Perhaps we can chat some other time."

"Let's do that."

"I'm here every day."

"We're one big family here," Dr. Corwin said as Rev. Pendragon continued on his way. "When I think of the patients being tossed into the street to fend for themselves...." His voice faltered. He was too choked up with emotion to say any more.

At last we were going to meet Ted Rodis. Or so I assumed when we rounded the corner into a large, open room, scattered with tables and chairs, which at first I took for the library. The walls were lined with shelves, though not, I quickly realized, with books—the shelves were crammed with board games and puzzles. Beneath a pair of high windows stood a dilapidated piano and a TV enclosed in what looked like an animal cage. "This," Dr. Corwin said with evident pride, "is our patient lounge."

Most of the patients must have been lounging somewhere else that day, possibly in their padded cells. Only one was in the lounge, a scrawny, stringy-haired blonde in a pink dress, aged somewhere between fifteen and fifty, who huddled on a folding chair with her knees drawn up to her chin as if trying to squeeze into the smallest possible space. In front of her a table was set up for a game of Clue. The board lay open, the characters—Mrs. Peacock, Colonel Mustard, Professor Plum—stood ready to begin their investigations. No tokens had been placed on the board announcing that the murder had been committed in the conservatory with a revolver, or in the billiard room with a lead pipe. In fact the patient—who I now realized was a young woman about my own age—hadn't rolled the dice or touched the cards. She wasn't playing but just sitting there staring at her knees.

She reared away from us in wide-eyed alarm. "That wasn't me talking," she said, though none of us had heard anyone speak. Her voice was small and constrained, as if being forced through a narrow opening.

"Who was it, then, Renée?" Dr. Corwin asked her with touching gentleness.

She shook her head, refusing to answer.

"Are they sending those TV signals again?"

She nodded fervently. "All the time. I don't know why they can't use someone else. Why do they have to use me?"

"Do you hear voices?" Borges asked.

"No," she said. "Always the same voice."

"What does it say?"

She glared at Borges with crazed curiosity. "You're blind, aren't you?" she shouted. "You're blind!"

Before Borges could react, a security guard entered the room and stumbled to a halt, apparently surprised to find us there. He was in his late forties, balding, with his stomach bulging out of his shirt front and the same fishlike stare as the orderly who'd overpowered me in the lobby. "Excuse me," he mumbled—and Renée jumped as if he'd fired a gunshot.

"Excuse me!" she echoed in a low, husky voice not at all like the one she'd used before. "Excuse me!"

Dr. Corwin soothed her with an indulgent smile. "Getting late," he said, turning to Borges. "Let's move on to the library."

He led us down another dingy corridor and through a heavy wooden door, and at last we entered the library. It was one big room, as far as I could tell, but shaped so you couldn't see it all at once, with alcoves and bifurcations that seemed to multiply forever. Book shelves ranged from floor to ceiling, reaching up two or three stories under the gabled roof, accessed by a system of catwalks linked together by a wrought-iron bridge that arched from one side of the room to the other. It was a relic of a bygone era, except for one startling anachronism: howling over it all were the strains of acid rock—specifically the Grateful Dead, whose first album had been released the year before. I'd listened to that record many times, in various states of intoxication. I'd never expected to hear it in a place like this.

In the midst of this pandemonium, behind the librarian's elaborate desk, sat Ted Rodis, bobbing his head to the music as he sorted an enormous pile of books and file cards. We were all philosophers in that Age of Aquarius—we'd invented sex, drugs and rock 'n' roll and we'd have a lot more to say before we were done—but Ted actually looked the part. With his dark, curly beard, his bright eyes, his open and engaging smile, he might have been a teenage Socrates or Spinoza, overflowing with ideas though too young for anyone to take him seriously.

Dr. Corwin introduced us and excused himself to attend to other patients. As soon as he was out the door, Ted leaned forward and aimed a suspicious smile at Borges. "Are you with the FBI?" he asked.

"The FBI?" Borges snorted. "What makes you think that?"

"You're no doctor. I'm sure of that."

Borges's grip on his walking stick tightened. I could feel him swaying beside me as he took umbrage at this insult. "I am Jorge Luis Borges," he said, nodding curtly. "Honorary Doctor of Literature, University of Cuyo, 1956."

At this, Ted Rodis roared a deep and all-embracing laugh that had more philosophy in it than a whole library of treatises. He rushed forward and embraced Borges, sitting the old man down across from him at the desk. "Now that's the kind of doctor I need!" he declared. "Why didn't they send you in sooner?"

"They seem to think you need the other kind," Borges said. "They consider you a madman."

"I can hardly blame them," Ted smiled. "The only difference between myself and a madman—as Salvador Dalí likes to say—is that I am not mad."

Not surprisingly, it turned out that Borges and the mad philosopher had a lot in common. While I wandered around the library pulling random books off the shelves—the collection seemed especially strong on insects, electric trains and stamp collecting—the two metaphysicians plunged into a discussion of Berkeley and Hume, Kafka and Cervantes, Schopenhauer and Nietzsche. And like a good therapist,

Borges kept bringing the conversation around to the patient.

"Everybody, all my life, has told me I have psychological problems," Ted confessed to Borges. "My parents, my teachers, guidance counselors, doctors— everybody. And for a long time I believed them; I thought I was totally screwed up. But then I started reading philosophy—Plato, Descartes, Spinoza, Kant. And I realized: I don't have psychological problems—I have *philosophical* problems. The same problems philosophers have been wrestling with for centuries, the same problems *anybody* would have if they thought seriously about the world for more than fifteen minutes."

"Such as?"

"How do I know the world is still there when I close my eyes? How do I know it will be there when I open them again?"

Borges shrugged. "Those questions no longer vex me."

Ted missed the reference to Borges's blindness. "In college," he went on, "they told me that reality is billions of infinitesimal particles flying around at the speed of light, but that wasn't what I saw when I looked at the world. I couldn't even *imagine* the reality that science claims is in front of us every minute of our lives."

"Did you finish college?"

He shook his head. "They said I was crazy when I rejected their picture of the universe. I wrote some of my ideas on a physics exam and they sent me to the counseling office. From there it was all downhill."

"You dropped out?"

"Turn on, tune in, drop out!" Ted laughed.

I understood what he meant, but I doubted if Borges did.

"Look," Ted went on, "instead of billions of particles popping in and out of existence a billion times a second, isn't it more likely that all the things we perceive, and all the things we infer from science, are pieces of something bigger—of Something with a capital 'S'—and that Something is what really exists? I'm not talking about God or some other supernatural force. I'm talking about *Reality*. Something's really there, even if it's only me asking the question. And then you've got to ask: What is it? Is it mind or matter? Or some combination of the two?"

"What do you think?" Borges asked.

"The more I think about it, the more I'm sure it's one or the other—either mind or matter—not some combination. That's the dualist fallacy: the ghost in the machine." His voice faltered and a gleam of terror flashed in his eyes. "That's what they want you to believe."

Now we're getting somewhere, I thought—to the place where philosophy circles back to psychology. Paranoia was very much in the air in those days, fed by the Vietnam War, the assassinations, the drug culture, and the pervasive solipsism of our generation. In his absurd suspicion that Borges and I had been sent by the FBI, his dread of the "machine" and a mysterious "they" (somehow linked to dualism) who tried to control his thoughts, and even in his philosophizing itself—with its idea that there was a "Something" lurking behind the disparate events observed in everyday life—Ted had sounded many of the themes of contemporary paranoia. I had to wonder: Were these the delusions of a madman or the speculations of a normal twenty-year-old who'd run afoul of the law? Borges (who'd been known to espouse similarly bizarre ideas in his published writings) sat quietly and said nothing.

"The doctors can't solve my problems," Ted said, smiling again. "The greatest minds in history haven't been able to solve them. But I refuse to run away from them. I refuse to take the easy way out." He swept his hand in a wide arc, centering himself in the ineluctable logic of his captivity. "So here I am."

I stood a few feet from the desk, leafing through *The Boys' Book of Bug Collecting*, published in 1923, keeping one eye on Borges, the other on Ted. On the wall behind Ted's desk, between the speakers from which the fierce Gratitude of the Dead continued to blare from a tape deck, hung a framed painting—at least I assumed it was a painting—which had been covered with a large white towel. The towel was emblazoned "Property of Danvers State Hospital" (presumably to thwart discharged or escaping inmates who might want to take home a souvenir), and I assumed it had been hung there to protect the painting from damage. But as it happened, I was mistaken about both the nature of this object—it was a mirror, not a painting—and the reasons for its concealment: Ted Rodis shared Borges's abomination of mirrors.

"I presume that there are no mirrors in this library," Borges said.

Ted stared back at him warily. "Why do you say that?"

"A man of your discernment would surely have removed or covered them, for which I applaud you," Borges said. "I too abhor mirrors."

That was too much for me. "What do you have against mirrors?"

"Multiplicity is an illusion," Borges said, "and mirrors perpetuate that illusion, making space appear infinite when it is in fact nonexistent. Look in any mirror (if you can bear to) and tell me otherwise."

I slipped *The Boys' Book of Bug Collecting* back into its slot. What would happen, I wondered, if I uncovered the mirror and peered into it, as Borges suggested? Would I end up as crazy as he was? I was tempted to slip quietly out the library door and lock it behind me. And why not? If I left without the mad philosophers, they could shut themselves inside the lunatic asylum and forget about the real world altogether. They'd be as happy as non-existent clams.

"Do you think someone's trying to kill you?" Borges asked Ted.

"Are you kidding?" Ted shrugged. "This place is a labyrinth. There's no way out and no way in. Who could kill me in here?"

Dr. Corwin opened the door and slipped back into the library. He exchanged some pleasantries with Borges and gently informed Ted that it was time to return to his room. Ted didn't react well. In an instant he was transformed from an exuberant, iconoclastic philosopher into a whiny little boy. "But I wanted to show them around the library," he argued. "I wanted to take them up on the Bridge of Sighs."

That was his name for the iron bridge that spanned the catwalks, which could be reached only by mounting a spiral staircase at either end. "Can't do that," Dr. Corwin said, glancing at Borges. "Dr. Borges can't climb up there."

The doctor turned off the music playing on the tape deck, which upset Ted. I stood beside Borges to help him find his way out.

"Hope you enjoyed our library," Dr. Corwin said.

"Not as big as some you've been in, I'm sure."

"To a blind man," Borges said, "every library is infinite."

"Infinite?" the doctor laughed, searching Borges's face for a glimmer of irony.

"Infinite because, to one who can't see, it contains every book that was ever written, every thought the human mind is capable of."

Dr. Corwin stared at Borges for a long moment. Then he reached over and pushed a button on the wall, presumably to call for assistance.

"Reality is too big, too seemingly random for the human eye," Ted added. "Everything fits into a pattern, but only a few with special gifts can perceive it."

A shadow crossed Dr. Corwin's brow. "Conspiracy theories again, Ted?"

Mrs. White appeared at the door to take Ted back to his room, holding a hypodermic syringe in her right hand. Ted cowered like a whipped dog when he saw her.

"I could be bounded in a nutshell," Borges said, widening his sightless eyes, "and count myself a king of infinite space."

One more surprise awaited us as we retraced our steps through the hospital. In the lounge, the patient called Renée still huddled at her table, the Clue board spread in front of her as before. The security guard with the fishlike

eyes—his name, I later learned, was Caleb McWilliams—
hovered at her side, making odd gestures which Renée
seemed to ignore. When he saw us coming he hurried away
as if continuing on his rounds. Dr. Corwin called his name
and overtook him, and the two of them had a heated
discussion, but in such low, harsh voices that I couldn't
understand what they said. While this was going on, I
glanced down at the table where Renée sat and noticed
something that hadn't been there before. As everyone
knows except Borges (I had to explain this to him several
times), the game of Clue includes six tokens representing a
variety of weapons—a candlestick, a revolver, a dagger, a
lead pipe, a wrench, a rope—and the players accuse each
other of using these weapons to murder the victim, Mr.
Boddy, in particular rooms. When we passed through the
lounge the first time, the board had been bare, but now
there was a token in one of the rooms.

The sight of that small metal object on the Clue board
sent a shiver down my spine, and it made me do something
I wouldn't ordinarily have done: I reached down, picked up
the token, and stuck it in my pocket. I glanced at Renée to
see if she had noticed. She stared straight ahead, paying no
more attention to me than she'd been paying to the security
guard.

In the parking lot, I helped Borges across the drifting
snow and into the Galaxie. I started the engine but waited
to put the car in gear. There was something I needed to
show him before we drove down from Hathorne Hill. My
hand shaking, I pulled the token out of my pocket and
stared at it, though I already knew what it meant. Without a
word, I pressed it into Borges's hand.

"What's this?" he demanded.

"If there's a murder in this place, we know where it's going to be committed, and with what weapon."

He nodded as if he thought I should have stayed behind in the lunatic asylum. "We do?"

"In the library," I told him. "With a rope."

Borges must have caught my cold. He developed a bad cough and for the next several days was unable to leave his apartment. Though he was running a fever, he refused to see a doctor. His wife did what she could, but he asked for me, because what troubled him, he said, was not his physical discomfort but the state of his mind. He needed to talk. I sat with him most of the day and into the night. There were times when he seemed to ramble incoherently; I realize now that those were some of his most lucid moments. We talked about Greek tragedies, Chinese fairy tales, and Norse eddas. We talked about philosophy and poetry, and his conviction that there are only about a dozen true metaphors in any language. And we talked about Ted Rodis and his terror of what he called the dualist conspiracy.

"Perhaps it is my illness," Borges said one evening, propped up with pillows on the couch. "At night, when even the yellowish glow I perceive during the day has dimmed to utter blackness, I envision Ted Rodis tossing in his bed at the lunatic asylum, tormented by the fear that he's the soul of a machine utterly alien to his being, like a moth flitting about inside a lantern until the light is extinguished."

"No wonder he's terrified," I said.

"To be locked forever in a contraption—it could be a hospital bed or a prison cell or your own body—you can never escape from."

Always he brought the conversation back to Descartes and Spinoza. One evening, after his wife had retired to her room, he reached out and wrapped his clawlike hand around my wrist. Another storm had blown in from the northeast, unfurling sheets of freezing rain in front of the street lights. The wind whistled around the windows like a chorus of demons trying to force their way inside. In the half-darkness he looked old and pale, almost transparent. "Dualism is the world's oldest ghost story," he said. "The dualism of mind and body—the ghost story that so terrifies Ted Rodis—has a close cousin in the dualism of matter and spirit, which is its mirror image on an infinite scale."

I started to say something but he cut me off: "And which, to Ted Rodis, must be infinitely more terrifying."

A blast of wind shook the window pane, and a violent noise rattled through the room, as if the storm had forced its way inside. "And not only to Ted Rodis," Borges went on. "To the dualists of matter and spirit, God is the conscious mind of a material universe that operates according to immutable laws. He's locked up in it, just as Descartes's mind is locked up in his body—the ultimate ghost in the machine."

I could hardly believe what I was hearing. Was this one of Borges's cosmic jokes, or did he expect me to take it seriously? "Are you suggesting that God—if there is a God—would be terrified by his own creation?"

"Of course not," he smiled. "Could there be a greater blasphemy than to believe in such a God? It was for this reason that Spinoza posited a monistic material universe that is identical with God."

"Pantheism?" I suggested.

"Atheism, his detractors called it. Atheism is often—some would say always—necessary to avoid blasphemy."

The days and nights passed and Borges's condition improved, to the point where he was planning a return to the coffee shop. We hardly talked about Ted Rodis or Danvers State Hospital anymore, and I seldom thought about them, except when I drove home on the back roads and happened to glimpse the hospital's dreary shape in the distance and remembered Renée's prediction of a murder with a rope in the library.

And then late one morning came the call from Mike Petro. Ted Rodis had been found hanging from the iron bridge that arched across the library.

They were calling it suicide.

∞

This is one of the parts of my autobiography I'd like to rewrite by remembering it differently, but when the muse slips into my bed and tells me her tales, I can't get the image of Ted Rodis hanging from that footbridge out of my mind. Was that the only way he could escape the terror of dualism—by either freeing his mind from its cage or strangling it back into the elements? I didn't understand Ted's terror then, but I do now. When I open my eyes in the morning, I feel like Ariel imprisoned in his cloven pine, held motionless for a dozen years, or like a child at the controls of an unwieldy machine, not a shiny well-oiled one but a rusty old clunker like my Ford Galaxie (which made it almost to twenty before it gave up the ghost). Until my pain medicine kicks in, the mind/body problem is no mere conceit of philosophers: it imposes itself on me with an intensity that would have terrified Descartes. *Je souffre, donc je suis:* I feel pain, therefore I exist—even, as has often happened since the accident, when I wish I didn't.

Three mornings a week at nine, Nilsa arrives to give me my physical therapy. She comes from Nicaragua, so, according to Ingrid, the smell coming from under the sink doesn't bother her. Nevertheless she has offered to help me find someone to fix the pipe. The landlord remains incommunicado, and Ingrid and Gracie are hoping that the smell will propel me to assisted living. "Have you called the landlord yet?" Ingrid asked the last time she was here.

I've never been able to resist teasing Ingrid. "I'm beginning to think there might not be a landlord," I told her.

"Of course there's a landlord," she said. "A building has to have an owner, doesn't it?"

"Maybe we're the owners," I suggested. "The tenants, I mean. Maybe each of us—"

"That would be a condominium," she cut me off. "You don't have a deed to your apartment, do you? Or pay taxes on it? No, because this is a regular apartment building. There has to be a landlord."

"I don't know why."

"Somebody had to build the building, right?"

"A long time ago," I conceded.

"Well, the wind didn't just blow it together. And after it was built, somebody had to sweep the stairs, shovel the snow and do all the other things landlords do. So there must be a landlord. You need to get him over here to fix that pipe."

I agreed to continue my search, though I suspected the landlord was just a legal fiction rattling around in the county real estate records. The chances of getting someone to repair the pipe were about as good as getting Ingrid to stop complaining about it.

Nilsa—sweet, lovely Nilsa—had a more practical suggestion. "When is the rent due?" she asked me after Ingrid left.

"First of the month."

"Don't pay it," she smiled, "and see what happens."

∞

Sometimes, like Ted Rodis, I try to imagine that what I have are philosophical problems. I try to imagine that the world goes away when I close my eyes. No such luck: with my eyes closed the pain only gets worse—it never goes away. It's my destiny, outside of me and yet a part of me, like my reflection; a thing of darkness I must acknowledge mine. In that reflection, in the middle of the night, I see an old man remembering how Borges abhorred mirrors. The idea of each generation duplicating the previous one—the beauty and the horror of that—appalled Borges. In Ingrid and Gracie I see their mother and I want to cry. And sometimes I think about poor Ted Rodis, dangling from that footbridge in the library, with his eyes open. A suicide, they said.

The Madman in the Library (Concluded)

We drove out to Danvers State Hospital as soon as we learned of Ted Rodis's suicide. A tearful Mrs. White escorted us into Dr. Corwin's office, and I was moved to see how deeply the tragedy had affected him. He looked ten years older than he'd looked before, with hollow cheeks and sunken, bloodshot eyes. Without a word, he offered us the chairs in front of his desk. I reached across to shake his hand

Borges kept both his hands balanced on top of his walking stick. "We were very sorry to hear about Ted," he said. "Such a tragedy."

"Very sad," Dr. Corwin agreed, his voice cracking with emotion. "Fine young man." He set his jaw defiantly. "Not fair to blame the staff. Nobody's fault."

"Is someone blaming them?"

"Police were here earlier. Questioned Mrs. White, the orderlies, security guards. Very upsetting."

"Do the police think this could have been prevented?"

Dr. Corwin shrugged and looked away. "Not much they could have done, was there? Had the boy on suicide watch."

That made us sit up and listen. "Really!" Borges exclaimed. "Why?"

"Liked to compare himself to Socrates. Loved life but wasn't afraid of death, he said. Claimed death doesn't exist. Not real, you know."

"It seems real enough now," I said.

"Yes, very real for those he left behind."

"Will there be an autopsy?"

"No need for that. Being cremated tomorrow."

We all sat quietly for a moment. "Could you tell us what happened, exactly?" Borges asked.

"Hanged himself in the library. From the iron bridge he called the Bridge of Sighs. Early this morning, probably about six o'clock. In there by himself with the door locked."

"Are you the one who found the body?"

"No," Dr. Corwin frowned. "Security guard. Caleb McWilliams. Worked here all his life."

"Where did Ted get the rope?"

"Wish I knew. Nothing resembling a rope is allowed in this facility."

"Did he leave a note?"

"Haven't been able to find one. Searched high and low."

I was a little embarrassed at the way Borges kept pressing the doctor with his questions. Evidently the favorable notices he'd received for his first venture into detective work had gone to his head. "When I spoke to Ted," he continued, "suicide seemed to be the farthest thing from his mind."

Dr. Corwin nodded in agreement. "What do you make of it, then?"

"I see it as a classic locked room mystery," Borges replied. "The victim is found in a locked room—I assume it was locked from the inside—with no means of entrance by the murderer."

"No reason to think it was murder," Dr. Corwin said, shaking his head.

"Yet it's an arresting image, don't you think? Poor Ted trapped in that room like a ghost in a machine?"

"A ghost in a machine?"

"You'd agree," Borges smiled, "that there's a resemblance between a locked room mystery and the mind/body problem? I doubt very much, in Ted's case, if that resemblance is coincidental."

"Not following this at all," Dr. Corwin mumbled. His eyes pleaded with me for an explanation. All I could do was smile back to show my sympathy for his plight. He wasn't the first person who'd been lost in one of Borges's labyrinths.

"We're making progress," Borges said. "Now, in any locked room mystery the first question is whether the victim was in there alone. I assume Ted entered the library from the door we went in last week?"

"Yes. Went in there all the time."

"At six in the morning?"

"Unusual but not unheard of. Had the run of the place."

"And he bolted the door from inside?"

"That's right."

Borges leaned forward as if to peer into the doctor's eyes, which in fact were focused on me. "I must ask you: Was there was another way into the library?"

"Well, yes," Dr. Corwin said, to my surprise. "Heating tunnels all over the place. And one of the outside doors was found unlocked."

"Did it lead in to the library?"

"Indirectly, yes. Don't know if anyone came in or not. Security guard was supposed to be checking the doors."

"Caleb McWilliams?"

Dr. Corwin nodded.

"So someone could have come in from outside, such as Mel Lyman or one of the hippies from his commune that Ted was so worried about?"

"I suppose so."

"What was he afraid of?"

"Mel Lyman's a major drug trafficker," Dr. Corwin said. "When he's not being God. FBI picked Ted up, he talked a little too much. Thought Lyman would come after him. To shut him up."

"Did you believe any of that?"

Dr. Corwin shook his head. "Paranoid rubbish, as far as I was concerned."

Borges seemed to agree. "What about someone who works here? Could one of the orderlies, for example, have gone out and come back in through that door?"

"I suppose so. Never thought of that. But... the orderlies? That's ridiculous!"

"Just one possibility out of many," Borges said, waving his hand dismissively. "The mere possibility that someone entered through that door has undermined one of the ironclad assumptions of the locked room mystery. It appears that Ted might not have been alone in the library."

"Quite right," Dr. Corwin agreed.

Of course it was Borges, not Dr. Corwin, who'd characterized the matter as a locked room mystery. All the doctor had said was that they found Ted in the library by himself with the door locked. Now, as Borges spun out his fantastical analysis, Dr. Corwin smiled and nodded with unflappable politeness. Evidently he was accustomed to humoring crazy people.

"Of course there's another possible solution to the locked room problem," Borges went on. "The possibility that the murder was committed from a distance—in other words, by someone not present in the room."

"From a distance? How could that be?"

"Don't you ever watch television? The images you see on your screen have traveled a great distance to inflict a dangerous, potentially fatal injury to your brain."

We all had a good laugh at that, though I knew Borges wasn't joking. "Action at a distance," he added, "includes distance in time."

"Distance in time?"

"A delay, in other words. Was there anything that happened *before* Ted went into the library that could explain what happened? Did anything unusual happen the day before?"

"Well, yes. His father came for a visit. Afternoon before Ted died."

That woke me up. Ted's father—who'd kicked the magazines off his own coffee table when Borges tried to explain philosophical idealism to his wife—had visited Ted shortly before his death. Could he have brought him the rope?

Borges inhaled sharply and leaned forward with his hand on his walking stick. He had the air of a hawk about to snag his prey. "His father? Did he go into the library? Was he alone?"

"Alone, yes. The mother didn't come. Just the father. In the library, yes. They had quite an argument in there."

"An argument? About what?"

"Couldn't say. Left them alone in there for a while to take care of another patient. You think his father might have something to do with this? Absurd!"

"Mr. Rodis returned home that afternoon?"

"Oh, yes. Definitely went home. Inconceivable. Rubbish."

Dr. Corwin had grown increasingly flustered and incoherent as Borges probed deeper into his account of Ted's death. Of course if it was suicide, as Dr. Corwin assumed, none of these inconsistencies made any difference, so he could be forgiven for overlooking them. Despite a wealth of experience with paranoiacs, Munchausens and megalomaniacs, he had certainly never encountered a fabulist of Borges's gifts, who could discern cracks in the very foundations of the universe if they were needed to tell a good story. And it was consistent with what I'd observed of Dr. Corwin's genial character that he would have a difficult time imagining the evil machinations implied by Borges's questioning.

"Were there any other visitors that afternoon?" Borges asked.

"No. The reverend, of course."

"Reverend Pendragon?"

Dr. Corwin smiled sympathetically. "Yes. But he—"

"But what?"

"Well, he saw Ted every day. Had their philosophical differences, of course. Almost came to blows on one occasion."

"The reverend?"

"Got a temper. But so did Ted, you know."

"All right, then," Borges pursued. "Were there any other unusual circumstances involving Ted in the twenty-four hours before he died?"

Dr. Corwin's eyes wobbled, as if he were observing his office for the first time. He plucked a book from the clutter of his desk, pretended to examine it, and set it back down in a slightly different location. "Actually there was," he mumbled. "Didn't think it mattered. Suicide, you know. Absurd to think."

"What was it?"

"Young woman. In the patient lounge the day you were here, I think. Renée is her name. Very pretty girl."

"What about her?"

"Found her—Floyd Akers, one of the orderlies, found her—in Ted's room that morning. Right after they found Ted."

"In the library?"

"No, in Ted's room."

This revelation gave me a secret shudder which I shared with Borges, though neither of us showed any reaction. We'd agreed not to mention Renée or the token she'd left on the Clue board, foreshadowing a murder in the library with a rope. We were determined to question her about that ourselves.

"What was she doing in Ted's room?" Borges asked.

"Floyd Akers found her in there," Dr. Corwin said. "Curled up on his bed with her face to the wall."

"How did she get in there? Were she and Ted friends?"

"Friends, yes. Could say that."

I thought I could hear something more than usually evasive in that answer. "What else could you say?"

"Troubled girl, Renée." He picked up a pencil and fidgeted with it for a moment. "Notorious for offering sex to the male patients."

"Could she have been involved in Ted's death?"

"Can't see how."

"Maybe she went to the library with him. Maybe she saw him jump off the bridge. Maybe she pushed him."

"Very troubled girl," Dr. Corwin murmured. "Not violent, though."

"When can we talk to her?" Borges asked.

"We're keeping her in her room. Suicide watch."

"Are all the patients on suicide watch?"

Dr. Corwin attempted a smile. "Tend to run in clusters, don't they?"

A few minutes later we were on our way down the hall to see Renée. "Former graduate student in philosophy," Dr. Corwin told us. "Quite brilliant, I understand. Became a drug addict, then worked as a prostitute to support her habit. Bad situation all round. Suffered a severe schizophrenic reaction and had to be hospitalized. Sweet girl for all that. Very sad story."

Dr. Corwin's eyes glistened with the compassion I'd observed when he spoke about Ted. "Very sad," he repeated, stopping at a windowless door with a number on it. He unlocked the door with his key and knocked softly. When there was no response, he nudged the door open and motioned us inside. "Word to the wise," he murmured. "With Renée you don't always know who you're talking to."

The doctor disappeared down the hall, leaving us alone with Renée. Borges tugged on my sleeve. "You do the talking," he said, smiling ironically. "I'll observe."

Renée's "room" looked like a padded cell to me. It contained a frameless bed, a washstand and toilet and very little else. The faint glow of winter light from one window high on the wall was the only evidence of an external world. Renée looked as pale and insubstantial as a wraith, wrapped in the same pink dress we'd seen her in before. She crouched on her bed, her back to the corner with her knees almost touching her chin. She didn't seem to see us come in. When we introduced ourselves, she smiled and nodded but gave no sign that she remembered us. She spoke in a soft, little-girl voice that sounded like a talking doll. After some small talk, I brought the subject around to what had happened the night before Ted Rodis died.

"Did you sleep with Ted that night?" I asked her.

"Sleep? No, we didn't sleep."

"Did you have sex with him?"

She shook her head. "All he wanted to do was talk."

"What did you do?"

"It was getting late—early, I mean. The sun would be coming up soon." Her voice had deepened to a smooth, sensuous purr that sounded as phony as the talking doll. *"Come on,* I said. *Your time's almost up. Aren't you even going to touch me?"*

"What'd he say?"

"I only want to touch your soul."

In the late Sixties, that was what passed for a beautiful thought. But Renée didn't see it that way. "Isn't that ridiculous?" she laughed, her voice suddenly brittle with scorn.

"Why?"

"Nobody can touch your soul. Only our bodies can meet."

"Our bodies?"

"That's all any of us are"—she dropped into a hoarse growl that was unlike any of the voices we'd heard before—"Bodies. The rest is just messages they send through the TV."

An image of Ted Rodis's lifeless body dangling from the iron bridge flashed across my mind. I thought of Mr. Boddy, the name of the victim in Clue. "You put the token on the Clue board, didn't you, Renée?" I asked her gently. "How did you know what was going to happen?"

She wrapped her arms around her knees and rolled up into a ball.

"Do you know who gave him the rope?"

She spun away from us and wedged her face into the corner.

Borges was uncharacteristically quiet as I drove him home that afternoon. He jiggled his walking stick, sighed—at times I even thought I heard him humming a tune—but said nothing all the way back to Cambridge. I was quiet as well, a little too lost in my own thoughts to be driving a car, especially the Galaxie, which needed careful supervision. "If Ted's death was murder," I found myself muttering, "there's no shortage of suspects."

"Name them," Borges commanded.

"All right," I said. "Renée, who predicted how and where the murder would be committed. Ted's angry father, who visited him the afternoon before he died and could have brought in the rope. Rev. Pendragon, who had philosophical differences with Ted and a surprising bad temper. Caleb McWilliams, the guard who discovered the body after leaving the exterior door ajar. Floyd Akers, the fish-faced orderly who almost went ballistic at the mention of Ted's name. Mrs. White, the nurse who made Ted cower when she arrived to take him back to his room. Not to mention the mysterious Mel Lyman and his hippie followers, the FBI, the dualists—"

"That's enough!" he cut me off. "In a detective story there must not be more than six suspects."

"But this isn't a story," I objected. "This is"—I hesitated to say it—"reality."

"Nonsense!" he scoffed. "Do you suppose that the canons of literature are arbitrary conventions? That when Aristotle says a tragedy must have a beginning, a middle and an end, he's merely indulging his personal taste?"

"No, not in that case, but—"

"That he could have imposed any number of other requirements, such as breaking a leg or falling off a cliff? Those are misfortunes, not tragedies, and no amount of philosophizing by Aristotle could have made them otherwise."

"But —"

"Archetypes are the very form of the reality you so blithely invoke. And in the case of detective stories, the rule is clear. There can only be six suspects."

We drove on, quiet again, and I took the opportunity to think about a few issues in my own life. My course work at Ipswich was not going well, my apartment was infested with cockroaches, and my love life was non-existent. The Galaxie itself was wearing down; I could envision a time, not far in the future, when it would collapse into a cloud of dust. That cloud might have a silver lining, if it meant I could resign from my post as Borges's chauffeur. But he wouldn't stand for it, I knew that; and I would miss those morning feasts in Somerville, where I could look forward to plenty of black coffee, cheese danishes, and the lovely Diotima.

Borges must have spent the drive thinking about his six suspects, but he had nothing to say about any of them except Renée. When I pulled up in front of his apartment house, he sat and waited for me to help him out of the car. "The key to the case is the relationship between Renée and Ted," he said. "Why was she in Ted's room that morning?"

"Supposedly they were friends. Maybe even lovers."

"They made the perfect couple, like Berkeley and Hume. He denied the body, she denied the soul."

"She ridiculed him for wanting to touch her soul."

"Renée is a courageous woman," Borges said, "a living rebuke to Descartes—she doubts the existence of her own mind. Which may be the reason she has lost it."

I wondered if such radical doubt could be related to Dr. Corwin's unusual capacity for sympathy with his patients. Sometimes, I've been told, a patient will assert a belief—or even feign a psychosis—simply in order to thwart the therapist's attempts at a cure, which the patient perceives as an insult, an invasion of privacy, or a rejection. "It's a cunning tactic for a mental patient," I said, "to deny that she has a mind."

Borges nodded. "Even more so for a prostitute."

We were invited to attend a memorial service at the hospital a few days later. It was a gray, humid morning, warm enough to raise a fog over the melting snow. Borges rode quietly in the back seat, steadying himself with his cane as I piloted the Galaxie over the twisting roads. The loss of his eyesight had left him with an uncanny sense of time and place. He knew the exact moment when we reached Hathorne Hill, and he gasped, as I did, when the grim silhouette of the asylum rose out of the mist. "What the judges in the Salem witch trials were grappling with was essentially a locked room mystery," he said, with apparent sympathy.

"They were?" I asked.

"It was the seventeenth century, the century of Descartes and Spinoza, but also of Puritanism, predestination, Milton and Donne. Everyone believed in witches: the judges, the accusers, even the accused. You can hardly blame them for seeking solace in one of the classic solutions."

"The classic solutions? Solutions to what?"

"To a locked room mystery. And the solution, of course, was action at a distance."

"What are you talking about?"

Borges's voice was impatient, almost patronizing. "You're aware, I assume, that most of the accusations of witchcraft involved spectral apparitions?"

"I wasn't aware of that," I admitted. In fact I couldn't remember the last time I gave spectral apparitions a second thought. I didn't even know what they were.

"The accusers typically swore that they *saw* the witches who tormented them and could identify them by name, no matter that their assailants were miles away at the time. And this sinister touch—the notion that, spurred on by the devil (with God's consent, of course), the witches could perform their evil work at a distance, through locked doors—was what sealed their doom."

I slipped the Galaxie into a parking space in front of the hospital, stunned by the breathtaking presumption of his parenthetical. "What do you mean, *with God's consent?*"

"The Puritans' God knew everything and controlled everything. They would never have supposed that such deviltry could go on without his knowledge and consent. Anyone who suggested otherwise would have been branded a heretic and burned at the stake."

"That's not my idea of what God would be if I believed in him."

"Nor mine. But neither can I envision an impotent God, with no jurisdiction over evil in this world or the next."

I turned to face him, searching his clouded eyes for signs of irony. "Do you believe in the next world?"

"You know me better than that," he chuckled. "I don't even believe in this one."

The memorial service—in what seemed a shocking lapse of good taste—was held in the library, where Ted had died just five days before. A pump organ was rolled in for the occasion, and Mrs. White, bursting at the seams of her spotless nurse's uniform, performed a medley of lugubrious hymns. Borges and I arrived at the last minute, escorted by Dr. Corwin, who'd met us at the front desk. When we reached the library, he excused himself to attend to the other mourners. The family stood to one side, near the librarian's desk: Ted's mother, sobbing into her handkerchief. His father, jaw set, eyes down, trying to avoid looking in our direction. His uncle Mike Petro, stolid, wary, still in need of a shave; he nodded gravely as we walked in.

The other side of the room, where the patients gathered in their hospital garb, looked like a pajama party in search of a padded cell. The patients huddled around the refreshment table, shoving cookies into their mouths, stuffing them in their pockets, dropping them into the Kool-Aid bowl. When Borges and I, in our dark suits, appeared beside the table, they took us for caterers and began peppering us with outrageous questions and demands. I noticed Renée, in her pink dress, wrapped around a folding chair like a terrified flamingo.

Patrolling between these groups was Floyd Akers, the sullen orderly who, by some accounts, had never set foot outside the hospital. "You!" he sneered when he saw Borges and me. "You came to visit Ted Rodis once." Even at Ted's funeral he made no effort to conceal how much he hated him.

"What did you have against Ted?" I asked him.

"He didn't respect me," he snarled. "Told the reverend"—he nodded toward the elderly chaplain we'd met on our first visit—"told the reverend I didn't exist when he closed his eyes."

"It wasn't personal," Rev. Pendragon said, shuffling up beside me in his black coat and clerical collar. "He was talking about the whole world. I was just using you as an example."

"Well, I took it personal." Floyd bared his teeth in what I hoped was a grin. "Now his eyes are closed for good, and I'm still here. What do you make of that?"

"God's ways are not our ways," the reverend muttered.

At the far end of the room, blocking the spiral staircase that mounted to the Bridge of Sighs, stood Caleb McWilliams, the security guard who'd discovered Ted's body. He shared Floyd's amphibian appearance—I later learned it was common to natives of Innsmouth—and with a sinking feeling I remembered the scene in the patient lounge when he seemed to hover over Renée, possibly making inappropriate advances, and then I recalled that it was Floyd who'd discovered Renée in Ted's bed the morning he died, in her usual catatonic state, and it sickened me to think that either of those chthonic throwbacks might have laid a hand on Renée. I wondered if Ted Rodis had experienced the same feelings and tried to protect her from those brutes.

At a signal from Dr. Corwin, the organ music swelled to a climax and ended on a bright major chord. Mrs. White clapped the keyboard shut and marched to the refreshment table, where she herded the patients into folding chairs to keep them away from the cookies and Kool-Aid during the ceremony. I pictured her as I'd glimpsed her that day we talked to Ted, waiting to take him back to his room. What was in that syringe that so terrified him? Undoubtedly one of the many drugs an autopsy would have found in his bloodstream, if anyone had done an autopsy.

I assumed that Rev. Pendragon would conduct the ceremonies, but instead it was Dr. Corwin who raised his voice and asked that everyone join in a moment of silence. When that moment had passed, he unfolded a piece of paper and read something that Ted had written several weeks before, a meditation on life and death and the mystery of the cosmos. It wasn't exactly a prayer (appropriately enough for a pantheist—what's the point of praying to everything in the universe, including yourself?) but it was prayerful and spiritual, and it was appreciated by Ted's mother, who responded with a round of sobbing. Dr. Corwin, in his awkward but gentle way, said all the things you'd expect to hear on such an occasion. We were here to celebrate Ted's life, not his death. Life is a gift, and Ted's life cast a light that brightened those of everyone around him. "The mind's a wonderful thing," Dr. Corwin concluded. "Most wonderful thing in the universe. Can spend your life inside it"—he waved his hands in a circle, as if he were talking about the library—"but to everyone else it's like a locked room. We can try to help you get out of that room. At least for a visit. But sometimes the best thing is to stay inside. Sometimes it's best to just stay inside."

Dr. Corwin asked if anyone would like to share their memories or feelings about Ted. Ted's father stood up to speak, but the poor man was too choked up to say anything. "I feel your pain," Dr. Corwin said, nodding sympathetically. "Let's take a few minutes to comfort each other for our loss. And then we'll all have another chance to share our feelings."

At a signal from Mrs. White, the patients launched another assault on the refreshment table. Rev. Pendragon sidled up beside Borges with a cup of Kool-Aid in his hand. "We Unitarians believe that there is, at most, one God," he told Borges. "And I'm confident that God, if He or She exists, will be smiling down on us today."

Borges could hardly contain his excitement at having met a Unitarian. "Emerson was a Unitarian!" he exclaimed.

"Surely you're thinking of Thoreau," the minister corrected him.

"No, sir, I—"

"Yes, I'm quite certain you're thinking of Thoreau. Emerson was the one who lived out in the woods."

The reverend elbowed his way past the incredulous poet to snag another cup of Kool-Aid off the table. To have been interrupted—and then to have been corrected, erroneously, on a point of literary biography—was almost more than Borges could bear. He stiffened on his walking stick, suppressing his rage, as Rev. Pendragon changed the subject to Ted Rodis. "Such a tragic, meaningless death," the reverend said, shaking his head.

"Of course," Borges said coldly. "The very meaning of death, if it has one, is meaninglessness."

Rev. Pendragon's brow darkened. "How very cynical!"

"In cynicism there is hope," Borges said, smiling maliciously.

Rev. Pendragon frowned and wandered away with his hands folded in front of him, as if trying to think of a Unitarian prayer.

"I wrote a story once," Borges said, turning to me, "about a vast, possibly infinite library that might have been the universe. No book in the library, or even a single page in any book, made sense to the librarians who worked there. The books appeared to be composed of random arrangements of letters. Yet the librarians believed that if they could somehow see the library as a whole—if they could read *all* the books—they would begin to grasp a pattern and their world would have order and meaning."

"Did they ever find what they were looking for?"

"No, of course not," he chuckled. "Did I mention that the library was quite possibly infinite?"

At the other end of the refreshment table, Rev. Pendragon was raising a ruckus. "I wanted Hawaiian punch, I told you!" he yelled at Mrs. White. "Not Kool-Aid!" He hurled his plastic cup down on the table. "And peanut butter cookies! I told you I wanted peanut butter cookies!"

Dr. Corwin glided toward the table with a menacing Floyd Akers at his side. "Now, Luther," he said in a soothing voice. "Got to behave yourself in here. Can't control yourself, have to ask Floyd to take you back to your room."

I shook my head in disbelief. "Reverend Pendragon is an inmate!" I told Borges.

"I suspected as much," Borges said. "Only a madman would confuse Emerson and Thoreau." We later learned that his name was Luther Bigelow and he'd been committed to Danvers some thirty years before. Not only wasn't he a clergyman, but (as Borges took great satisfaction in determining) he wasn't even a Unitarian.

At last Dr. Corwin called for everyone's attention and proclaimed another moment of silence. "Before we conclude," he said, "time for everyone to reflect. Anyone who wants to say anything. Something you remember about Ted. Or just how you feel. Anything at all you'd like to say."

Ted's father stumbled forward again, choking with emotion. "I just want to say," he stammered, "Ted was my son and sometimes he didn't do what I wanted, he definitely had ideas of his own and I didn't agree with them, but he was a good kid, a loving son, kind to his mother, he always reached out to help someone if he could. I'm so sorry I couldn't have stayed here with him that night."

Mrs. White ventured out from behind the refreshment table, keeping one eye on the patients. "Ted was a gentle soul who wondered if the world was still there when he closed his eyes. Now his eyes are closed forever and it's up to us to keep his dream alive."

Dr. Corwin beamed over the crowd. "Anyone else?"

A scuffling noise caught our attention as Renée untangled herself from her folding chair and stumbled across the room, smiling inappropriately at Mr. Rodis, who edged closer to his wife.

"No, Renée," Dr. Corwin said gently. "Don't think that's a good idea."

Renée shrank back as if trying to retreat, but the crowd had closed in behind her. "Go back to where you were sitting, Renée," Dr. Corwin said. "Mrs. White, would you help Renée, please?"

Borges tightened his grip on my elbow. "This is a voice we need to hear," he called out in his most authoritative voice. "Go ahead, young lady."

"No, Dr. Borges," Dr. Corwin said. "Not a good idea."

"Go ahead, Renée," Borges persisted. "We want to hear what you have to say."

"No, Dr. Borges." Dr. Corwin glared at Borges in exasperation. "Renée—"

"Renée," Borges said, "tell us how you knew there was a rope in the library."

"Ridiculous. Very sick girl. Floyd, take Renée back to her room."

"Where's the note, Renée?" Borges demanded.

"The note?" Dr. Corwin asked. "What are you talking about? There wasn't any note."

"Maybe Renée knows where it is."

Renée edged forward and to everyone's surprise she walked right past Dr. Corwin and stopped in front of the librarian's desk. She glanced tentatively at Borges, who of course couldn't see her. Then she reached behind the desk and pushed a button on the tape player. The keening of the Grateful Dead began to pulse through the room.

"You see!" Dr. Corwin crowed. "Nonsense. Very sick girl. Turn that thing off!"

Renée stood still, as if transfixed by the music. She stared at Borges with an intensity that might have been painful if he'd been able to see her.

"My God!" he cried out. I think he was reacting to the music.

In the middle of a sinuous Jerry Garcia guitar solo, the music stopped. We heard a loud pop and the tape began to hiss. Then came voices, faint voices we couldn't identify or understand. Voices of men who seemed to be arguing.

"Turn it up," Borges told Renée. "Turn up the sound."

Renée reached down and turned the knob until the men could be heard clearly. Everyone recognized them— one was Ted Rodis and the other was Dr. Corwin.

"I care about you, Ted," Dr. Corwin was saying, in his soft, crooning voice. "No place for people like you out there. Don't you see? Eat you alive, they will."

"Don't take that out again," Ted pleaded. "Leave it in the drawer. I told you—"

"Show you what it's like up on the bridge," Dr. Corwin said. "Just stand there with this around your neck. Don't have to jump. Don't have to do anything. Just let me show you."

"No," Ted said. "Not today. I don't want to."

"OK, not today. Doesn't have to be today. Could be some other day, Ted. But you'll stand up there and see for yourself, won't you? Then you can decide for yourself."

"OK."

"Best for you, don't you see?"

All eyes turned on Dr. Corwin. No one dared to speak.

"Very sick girl," Dr. Corwin said, as if Renée were still the issue.

Ted's parents began to sob. Then Mrs. White started crying, followed by half the patients. Dr. Corwin nodded sympathetically, as he'd done when he said he felt their pain. When he was about to walk away, Mike Petro, who worked for the Essex County police, stepped forward and slipped a hand around his elbow. "I think you'd better come with me, Dr. Corwin."

Our drive back to Cambridge was pleasantly anticlimactic. I kept to the back roads, avoiding the icy patches, and made a mental note to stay out of lunatic asylums. Borges seemed more than usually satisfied with himself, taking full credit for solving the murder. "And make no mistake," he said, "it was murder, regardless of whether Ted jumped or was shoved off that bridge. A masterpiece of detection, even if I do say so myself."

"But didn't you violate the rules?" I objected. "You know, the six suspect rule? The killer wasn't Renée, or Ted's father, or Mrs. White, or the orderly or the security guard—"

"Those were your suspects, not mine," he scoffed. "I never considered Mrs. White a suspect, or any of the others for that matter. Certainly not that idiotic minister, who can't tell the difference between Emerson and Thoreau, or that foul-smelling orderly. And only a heartless cynic could have suspected Ted's father. Frankly, I'm surprised at you."

That cut me to the quick but I persevered: "What about Renée? Don't tell me you didn't suspect Renée!"

"Renée? Because she predicted a murder in the library with a rope? You might as well blame Cassandra for the fall of Troy."

Borges paused a moment to adjust his necktie, a sign that his fit of boasting had not run its course. "From the moment you told me about Renée's prediction," he went on, "I knew she was pointing at Dr. Corwin. Of course the murder still hadn't been committed. But as soon as it was, didn't you notice that all the evidence against your suspects came from Dr. Corwin? Ted never said he thought someone was trying to kill him—that was Dr. Corwin talking. The good doctor was always planting evidence against one of your suspects: they had enough motives, means and opportunities to stock a melodrama. Philosophical differences, heated arguments, underground passages, doors unaccountably left ajar—and if all else failed, they could kill at a distance, through locked doors, like spectral apparitions. In that hospital Dr. Corwin was the prime mover, and hence the prime suspect. Nothing went on there that he didn't let happen. As I first suspected, it was a locked room mystery. But Dr. Corwin didn't want us to know that, because he was the one with the key."

"But Ted outsmarted him in the end, didn't he?"

I meant to be ironic, but Borges, that master of irony, could never discern it in others. "Ted must have told Renée about Dr. Corwin's machinations with the rope," he said. "And he must have known that his death, however it occurred, would be treated as suicide. So he left a note that the doctor would never find, recording it over that horrible music, and told Renée where to look for it. She knew that her only chance was to play the tape when everyone was there for the memorial service."

"Clever girl, that Renée. Maybe I'll ask her out."

"By the way," Borges said. "That horrible music— what was it?"

"The Grateful Dead," I told him.

"The Grateful Dead." I could see him shaking his head in the rearview mirror. "A band of discordant dualists!"

"I doubt it. They're just a—"

He silenced me with a thump of his cane. "To be grateful that you're dead—that your material existence has ceased—may seem the ultimate rejection of dualism. Yet it implies a body, albeit a dead one, that is separate from the soul. I would like to ask this band of cacophonists: Who's going to be left to feel grateful after you're dead? Other than myself, of course."

Though Dr. Corwin eventually admitted that he forced Ted off the bridge with the rope around his neck, he insisted that he'd done nothing wrong. In this, as in similar incidents in the past—Ted was not his first victim—he had acted, he insisted, in the patient's best interest. Some people are simply not suited to life outside a maximum security residential psychiatric facility. Evidently the Commonwealth of Massachusetts decided that Dr. Corwin was one of those people. He later made his home in Bridgewater State Hospital, where he worked in the library and played Clue with some of his former patients, including Renée and (until his release) Rev. Pendragon. Dr. Corwin (now simply known as Jonathan) claimed that there was a book in the library that explained and justified all his actions, but no one was able to find it. According to Rev. Pendragon, who occasionally hit me up for spare change in Central Square, Renée predicted that one day there would be a murder in the patient lounge with a knife, and Jonathan would be the victim.

Borges and I soon slipped back into our routine of maté and De Quincey at the coffee shop in Somerville. The incomparable Diotima seemed glad to welcome us back. She winked knowingly when Borges said we'd been called away to handle a situation at Danvers State Hospital. Beyond that, neither of us mentioned the events of the previous two weeks. Our first morning back we sipped our drinks and talked about the weather and the hockey scores. The second day Borges lectured me on Dante and Cervantes, the third on Kafka and the Kabbalah. It was only after a week that we came back around to where we started. Borges insisted that I read the De Quincey essay to him again from the beginning. Though he could quote long passages from memory, he listened as if he'd never heard it before. Diotima stood near our booth, busying herself with needless tasks—wiping tables, filling salt shakers, replenishing napkin holders—so she could hear what I was reading.

De Quincey's claim that all philosophers are murdered, which I'd dismissed as a frivolity, had taken on a sinister, unsettling character, like a prophecy that had been fatally ignored. Even if it was not factual, Borges suggested, we had to acknowledge that in some sense it was true.

"All philosophers are the same philosopher," he said. "Just as all the blind men groping around the elephant are the same man."

"Why is that?"

"There's only one reality."

Diotima seemed relieved to hear this. With customers like us, she could be forgiven for wondering whether that issue was open to doubt.

There was no mention of Ted Rodis—his suffering was too recent to universalize, even to Borges—but it was understood that he had joined the immortal company of blind men around the elephant, shoulder to shoulder with Descartes and Spinoza and all the rest.

"I am saddened to think that Spinoza was murdered," Borges said. "As an amateur Platonist and a philo-Semite, I count Spinoza among the greatest of philosophers, especially since losing my sight. Spinoza's pantheistic God is like Poe's purloined letter, hiding in plain view. Invisible, unknowable, because he is everywhere and everything. He was present in the murder weapon, in the curses of the murderer, in Spinoza's dying screams. Just as Spinoza could not hide from his God, his God could not hide from him, in that final moment when both man and God must be judged."

∞

I felt sad about Ted, but less so about Spinoza, who, after all, had been dead for three hundred years. And Spinoza, by his own account, inhabited a deterministic world in which his own death was not only foreseeable but necessary, the last piece of a cosmic jigsaw puzzle snapping into place. I sympathized most with Renée, the materialist, who went mad doubting the existence of her own mind. I would have done the same thing if it meant I could feel no pain; instead I stayed in my locked room waiting for time to stop. At that point in my life it still seemed possible to be philosophical about death. Now—after Katie—I know that the only death you can be philosophical about is your own. I feel sorrier for Ted now than I felt then. I feel sorry for Spinoza even if he didn't feel sorry for himself. And I feel sorry for Achille Toulou and Stephen Albert and Mary Talbot—their tragedies lay ahead. I wish I could have stopped the clock before I ever heard their names.

In that event Katie would never have been part of my life—I can be philosophical about that. But then Ingrid and Gracie wouldn't be here, dropping by to help me with the shopping or scheduling appointments for all the rehab and physical therapy I've needed since the accident. Not that there would have been an accident, at least not that accident, or that I'd miss Ingrid and Gracie if they'd never been born, though I love them so; there would have been other daughters, sons perhaps, another wife, if that's conceivable, who'd probably still be alive. If at certain moments I'd stepped right instead of left... no, that could go on forever. This life was the only one I could have lived.

Gracie breezes in once or twice a week, laughing, chattering, making fun of my superfluous existence. She brings a momentary release from fate, while Ingrid, who visits more often, works hard to keep me in its clutches. Ingrid never leaves without giving me an assignment. The other day she introduced me to another tenant, a young man named Tom who lives in the apartment below mine. She made him promise to help me search for the landlord. "Tom knows where the realty management company is located," Ingrid told me. "He'll drive you over there so you can talk to them."

Tom is a stocky computer analyst who lives by himself and drives a Volkswagen Jetta. He's handsome, athletic and well-spoken, if not particularly interesting to talk to. I don't know how Ingrid recruited him or what he understands his mission to be. Is he supposed to aid my quest for the landlord or prove that it's an impossible dream? Will he drive me to the realty management company or to the Sunrise Assisted Living Center? If he wants to be helpful, why doesn't he just fix the leak and get it over with?

Tom has arranged for the two of us to visit the realty company on Friday. In the meantime I look forward to the visits from Nilsa, my massage therapist. If I could have a muse other than memory to light my midnight fancies, I would choose Nilsa. She's all fire and imagination, so young that she's barely touched by memory. She tells timeless stories of her country as she kneads my flesh with her strong, supple hands. Hers is the kind of assistance I need in the kind of living I want to do.

Borges was proud of his detective work—perhaps too proud—but he seemed increasingly troubled by its implications. Detectives work in the real world, a place Borges had seldom visited. Real crimes are committed there; real people bleed and die. The detective's job is to see that world as it is. Can he be a Platonist, a pantheist, an idealist? Can he believe in destiny—or in its opposite, which amounts to the same thing, blind chance? Or will he come to realize (and I think this had already started to happen to Borges) that his most cherished beliefs are forcing him into the complicity with evil he is so determined to resist?

In bed at night, when not bemused by memory, I try to listen to music but all I hear is time passing. Borges visualized the continuous bifurcation of time into a labyrinth of possible futures. With each breath, beginning with our first, we plunge deeper inside the labyrinth— there's no turning back. "Death is our only hope," he said one morning as we sat in the coffee shop. "Without death, all we'd have is infinity, which our minds can't comprehend."

"I'm glad you pointed that out," I said, slurping the last of my coffee. "For some reason, I've always been under the impression that death is a bad thing."

He shook his head vehemently. "Limitation is a condition of all understanding, and of all meaning."

Diotima offered to bring more coffee but I waved her away, for fear that she would overhear our conversation and have us committed. Borges had launched into a paean to the gods of Norse mythology, who loved death, he said, more than they loved life. Their destiny culminated in Ragnarök, the twilight of the gods.

"The Norse gods, far from being diminished, are more exalted because they are mortal," he said. "Their struggles have a meaning that is lacking in the Greek and Roman deities, who are reduced by their immortality to being capricious despots and frivolous fops."

I asked him what he thought of Wagner.

"Richard Wagner was a great criminal," he scowled, "who avoided punishment for his crimes by omitting to commit them. Nevertheless"—he tapped his ceramic maté straw on the table—"I owe him my first intimations of eternity. At sixteen, in Zurich, my mother made me sit through the entire *Ring* cycle."

"Was it Wagner's music that gave you your first glimpse of eternity? Or his dramatic vision of the gods—?"

"It wasn't the music," he waved his hand dismissively, "or the incoherent stew of depravity and metaphysics he attempted to dramatize. It was the sheer act of sitting through it. Under certain conditions, I realized, merely living from one moment to the next can take forever. There's a kind of immortality in that, albeit a temporary one. It's bound to end badly, like the Norse gods themselves— they die in the end. And for them, as for us, death comes as a blessing. Without it we would face an eternity of portentous leitmotifs and dissonances that never resolve."

∞

Time and death, death and time. The connection is at once obvious and occult. Sometimes, lying in bed at night, I feel like a condemned man whose only hope is to endlessly subdivide each remaining moment so the last one will never arrive. Borges thought of time as a bundle of discrete, unconnected moments that are linked through the fiction of the self. We need the self, he told me, to create the illusion that these fragments of time are bound together in a seamless flow. But if that's all the self is, why do we cling to it so vainly and tenaciously? In our next case—which I have chronicled as "Death and the Tortoise"—Borges found the limits of his vanity and discovered the tragic consequences that can follow from slicing time into smaller and smaller fragments. Many harrowing moments are recounted there, which no one would want to see extended or repeated. But an old man may be forgiven for asking: Why does time's arrow only fly in one direction? Why does it have to fly at all?

3.

Death and the Tortoise

It is all one to me where I begin; for I shall
come back there again in time.

Parmenides

One foggy morning I skipped my classes and drove
the twenty miles down to Cambridge to have
breakfast with Borges. We sat in our favorite
coffee shop, whose main attraction, from my point of view,
wasn't the eggs or the pastries—and it certainly wasn't the
coffee—but the charming Diotima, who seemed to have the
wisdom of the ages instilled in her dark eyes. It made my
day when she smiled at me.

"Diotima is as beautiful as ever," I observed as she
walked away.

Borges allowed himself a wan smile. "Blindness would
have made a Platonist of me even if I hadn't already been
one."

I felt like sinking into the floor. "Your blindness," I
stammered, "is a tragedy which—"

"There's nothing tragic about it." He silenced me with
a wave of his hand. "When a young man like you looks
around the room, a thousand things vie for his attention. I
don't have that problem. No matter where I look I see only

one thing: a luminescent golden haze, which represents everything you see in the world."

He turned toward the window and let the sunlight stream over his face. "As I sit here today, I'm ready to declare: The world consists of one thing and one thing alone—a golden haze. That's all that exists and all that has ever existed or will exist."

Diotima, returning with our cheese danishes, overheard the old man's outlandish declaration and shot me a quizzical glance, though she must have been used to Borges's speculations by now. I winked back at her, hoping to establish that I, at least, hadn't lost my grip on reality.

"You've heard of Zeno's paradoxes, no doubt?" Borges went on. "Achilles who can never catch the tortoise? The arrow that can never reach its target?"

"Sure," I lied.

"Zeno was mocking other philosophers who claimed that any quantity of space or time can be divided into an infinite number of subdivisions. In fact, as he showed, thinking about the world as more than one thing leads to absurdities. His paradoxes have never been refuted. Which means that my perception of the world as one big yellow haze is probably correct."

Borges sipped his maté as I flipped through the back pages of the *Record-American*, Boston's tabloid newspaper of that era, catching up on the sports news. "Speaking of Achilles," I said, "the papers are full of excitement about the upcoming marathon. One of the contenders this year is a Senegalese engineering student named Achille Toulou. The sportswriters always call him by his first name—it's French for Achilles—and tack on epithets like 'swift-footed' whenever they mention him. They think there's a chance he could come in under two hours."

Borges had no interest in sports, or anything else I read about in the newspaper. He sat facing the window, enjoying his maté and the golden haze. "No matter how fast that fellow runs," he chuckled, "he'll never catch up to the tortoise."

That conversation, in retrospect, took on a macabre light a few days later when Achille Toulou, training for the marathon on Concord Avenue in North Cambridge, was killed by a drunk driver. According to eyewitnesses, he twisted his ankle in a pothole and stumbled into the path of the oncoming car. Toulou died of his injuries the next day and the city went into a state of shock unequalled since the Kennedy assassination. The sportswriters dubbed the accident a "Greek tragedy" and called Toulou "the greatest runner since the real Achilles" (overlooking the fact that the real Achilles was a mythical character). They couldn't resist describing the stumble that led to Toulou's death as a "twist of fate," and of course there were many references to his Achilles heel. The mayor ordered flags to be flown at half-mast in his honor.

Borges was more philosophical. "The only reason this accident—otherwise a fairly routine event—is receiving this kind of attention is because of the runner's name. If his mother had named him George (as my mother named me), we would never have heard of him. Yet when she named him Achilles she was invoking a powerful archetype: the mythological hero, half human, half divine, a runner of preternatural ability with a vulnerable spot in his ankle that exposed him to all the hazards of mortality."

Diotima suppressed a mischievous smile and leaned over the table to refill my coffee cup. I kept my nose buried in the newspaper and she glided away.

"I wonder why he had to die along that lonely road," Borges mused. "Was it to fulfill a prophecy? Was that driver destined to seek out his fatal weakness?"

I shrugged. "Who knows?"

"What do your sportswriters say?"

"They're saying he lost the favor of the gods."

A week later Borges asked me to drive him and his wife to a reception being held in his honor by the Ibero-American Society of Greater Boston. I arrived at their apartment at seven o'clock and spent half an hour coaxing and cajoling them into the Galaxie. As usual, Borges spoke to me in English, seemingly for the purpose of excluding his wife from the conversation. Undaunted, she interrupted with phrases adapted from her Berlitz guide. "I beg your pardon, sir," she said as we sped down Memorial Drive. "Would you be so kind as to conduct us to the Copley Plaza Hotel?"

I made a soft landing on Boylston Street, in a zone reserved for limousines, and escorted the old couple toward the hotel entrance. Even allowing for their age and infirmities, they had a unique way of approaching their destination. Señora Borges would venture forward a few steps and then stop to wait for her husband. Borges, tapping his ivory-handled walking stick, would inch toward her, but before he reached her she would edge forward again and the process repeated itself. In all likelihood he would never have caught up with her if Ronaldo Pérez, the president of the Ibero-American Society, hadn't rushed out to greet them. He led them into the hotel at the same excruciating pace while I ran back to move the car.

The reception proved to be boring and—for the first couple of hours—utterly predictable. The hors d'oeuvres were tasteless, the speeches tedious, the chit-chat shallow and insipid. But late in the evening a series of incidents occurred that even Borges, with his surrealist leanings, could hardly have imagined. A Brazilian woman of mixed Portuguese and German descent named Renata Sousa de Alarcón—tall, blond and determined to be perceived as sexy in spite of her age, which must have been close to sixty— appeared beside him and slipped her slender arm around his waist. "How you've changed, Jorge!" she said in Spanish. That caught my attention: it was the first time I'd heard anyone call him "Jorge."

"Haven't we all," he frowned.

"You haven't been avoiding me, have you?"

He pulled her arm away and stumbled sideways into his wife, who seemed not to notice, being engrossed in a conversation she had memorized from her phrase book. "I trust I shall not be remiss in mentioning," Señora Borges was saying to a bald Mexican in a stylish blue suit, "that the favor of a reply is requested. Kindly obtain directions from my driver."

She meant me—several times that evening I heard her refer to me as her driver—but I paid no attention, straining to hear what the faded Brazilian beauty was whispering in Borges's ear. Renata Alarcón raised her whisper to an audible hiss: "I'll never forget you, Jorge. But you already knew that, didn't you?"

Suddenly her husband appeared at her side, a red-faced Argentine wine merchant named Hector Alarcón. He had overheard just enough of the conversation to become enraged with jealousy. He pulled his wife away and shook his fist at Borges, forgetting—or perhaps not knowing—that he was blind. "You'll pay for this!"

Señora Borges, now alert, shot Borges the kind of glance I hope never to see from someone I'm sharing a bed with. The guests crowded around in a circle, staring like cattle at a fence.

Borges flashed his warmest smile. "I can only hope that Señor Alarcón will reconsider his threats, at least for the time being. It is my lifelong ambition to be killed by a jealous lover, but not until I reach the age of ninety-five."

The conversation settled back into polite inanity with the arrival of Ronaldo Pérez, who rushed in to apologize for the behavior of the Alarcóns. Pérez was himself a poet—a "distinguished poet" was how he'd been described by one of the speakers—and he professed great admiration for Borges, though he mentioned several times during the course of the evening a certain review Borges had written in 1954, comparing his verse to the braying of a jackass. Pérez hinted that he expected Borges to apologize for that review, but Borges, for all his politeness, let it be known that he stood by every word he'd written. Before the discussion could degenerate into an argument, it was interrupted by a large, sweaty man with furtive eyes who carried a sheaf of jumbled papers in both hands. He bowed and introduced himself to Borges, in a grandiose, old-fashioned way, as Isidro Pla, a native of Havana, currently resident in Boston. Then he held his papers open in front of the blind man as if he expected him to examine them closely. "Do you recognize this story, Señor Borges?" he demanded in English. "I wrote it, but it should look familiar to you, since you've been plagiarizing it for thirty years. In case you don't remember: it's about a detective who gets lost in a labyrinth he doesn't understand until it's too late. There are four murders, corresponding to the four points of the compass—exactly four murders; could that be a coincidence?—each planned with meticulous cunning."

"If you wrote this story," Borges smiled, "you must know it better than I do."

"I wrote every word of it, I assure you!" The man began to circle Borges as he spoke, tossing an occasional glance at the hushed crowd that had gathered around us. Two security guards hovered at the rear of the crowd. "But then," Isidro Pla went on, "unlike you, I stopped, because it was enough to have written the right number of sentences, containing the right number of words, each with the right number of letters, all arranged in the right order with the right punctuation. I didn't show it to anyone, least of all to you. I didn't have it copied or printed. I didn't have it translated into twenty-six languages. And when I found this book in a second-hand book shop"—he held up a dog-eared copy of Borges's most popular collection— "containing my story, word for word (even though the meaning of those words, as I intended them, has nothing in common with your pretentious drivel), you can imagine my outrage! What an abomination! Let me make one thing clear"—he stopped circling and faced the crowd with a triumphant expression—"I have never authorized anything I've written to be published or printed in any form, and I never will. But this Borges! He has not only stolen my work, he has copied it into all the languages of Babel!"

Pla shook an angry forefinger in Borges's face and might have leapt on top of him if the security guards hadn't rushed forward to pull him away. They dragged him through the astonished crowd and out of the room. "I won't forget this!" he shouted as the door slammed shut.

All eyes were on Borges, who smiled serenely and waited for the din of conversation to resume. "Poor man!" he muttered. "I understand exactly how he feels."

"But he's completely insane!" I objected.

"He thinks I've copied his writings, and what is worse, that I caused them to be printed all over the world."

"Even so—"

"There's a kind of plagiarism that can drive a man insane," Borges said, his color rising as if he'd been tempted by that kind of insanity. "That nearly happened to me, in connection with the same story, which was plagiarized by another writer whose name will never cross my lips. To contemplate the limitless duplication of one's words is like staring into the abyss. You are repelled, almost nauseated, by the thought of this abomination, which is also the way I feel—the way I still feel, though I can no longer see—when I stand in front of a mirror. Repelled, not by the sight of my unprepossessing face, but by the thought of its duplication."

As we drove back to Cambridge, Borges seemed unusually nervous and voluble. It was clear that his encounter with the madman Isidro Pla had been the most memorable event of the evening. "That story about the four murders, which I wrote three decades ago, seems to have excited a great deal of interest in this country," he said. "There's a man in Ponca City, Oklahoma, named James DeMarce who believes that when I wrote that story I stole his soul. You heard me correctly: he thinks I stole his soul and somehow embedded it in that story. I didn't use his name (which I didn't know) or describe his face (which I've never seen). I have no idea what the resemblance is supposed to be. Nevertheless he has written me countless letters, in both English and Spanish, begging me to change the story or withdraw it from publication. He's threatened to sue me—for libel, for misappropriation, for casting him in an unfavorable light. I had to hire an attorney to sort all that out. Obviously Mr. DeMarce is delusional, probably insane; but as with Isidro Pla, I feel an unexpected kinship with him. We know each other only through the written word—in that sense he is a figment of my imagination, as I am of his. And yet I can't think of him without being overwhelmed by guilt. My story, he said in one of his letters, has caused him a lifetime of anguish."

The next morning, back in the coffee shop, Borges seemed to have forgotten about Renata Alarcón and Isidro Pla and even the madman in Oklahoma. All he wanted to talk about was Zeno and his ancient paradoxes. "One of the challenges with Zeno," he explained as he sipped his maté, "is that we don't have his original writings. All that has survived is the refutations—by Plato, Aristotle, and many others—and even with that advantage they are unconvincing."

My mind was foggy that morning and I had little interest in Borges's conundrums, which, after the absurdities of the night before, I was determined to avoid. I had picked up the *Record-American*, and my challenge, as I read the sports news, was to turn the pages so slowly that

Borges would assume he had my undivided attention. The Celtics were off to a miserable start, losing nine of their last ten games. Not that they were playing badly—it almost seemed that the better they played, the farther they sank in the standings, under a gaggle of teams that hardly belonged in the same league.

"Undoubtedly you are familiar with the paradox of Achilles and the tortoise?" Borges asked. "Achilles agrees to race the tortoise, and as a handicap he starts a hundred meters behind his competitor. The race begins and Achilles quickly runs to the point where the tortoise started. But by then the tortoise has lumbered ahead a few paces, and now Achilles must run to the tortoise's new position. By the time he reaches that point, the tortoise has proceeded a little farther, and when Achilles arrives at that point, the tortoise is ahead a little farther still—and so on *ad infinitum*. Since Achilles must always run to the spot the tortoise just left, he can never overtake him."

Borges had finally caught my attention. Did this mean the Celtics could never catch up to the Knicks? "No one in his right mind could believe that," I said. "What was Zeno trying to prove?"

"The impossibility—I would say the horror—of multiplicity."

"Multiplicity?"

Borges could scarcely conceal his glee at having lured me into a labyrinth I was determined to avoid. "If the universe can be sliced up into an infinite number of pieces, then nothing can change, because the pieces could always be smaller, and crossing even the narrowest gap between them would take an infinite amount of time. In a world of multiplicity, motion and change are impossible."

How had I allowed myself to be drawn into this so early in the morning? I tried focusing my mind back on the newspaper. A mutilated corpse had been discovered in a cemetery in Hyde Park, at the extreme southern end of the city. The police had no comment on possible motives for the crime.

"Surely you know the paradox of the arrow?" Borges pursued.

"Surely," I agreed, trying to finish reading the article.

"An arrow can never reach its target because first it must travel half the distance to the target, then half of that distance, and half of that distance, and so on, forever. Whatever distance remains can always be divided in half, and the first half of that distance must be crossed before the whole distance can be traveled."

"Of course." The victim had been identified as a high-school biology teacher from Medford. Married, with three children. Who would have wanted to kill such a man?

"The only solution is to recognize that the universe is a single, indivisible substance. Spinoza based his whole philosophy on this solution to Zeno's paradox. To Spinoza, the universe consists of only one thing, and that thing is God. God is not only everywhere, he is everything, the one unchanging substance of which everything in nature is only a variation."

I looked up from my newspaper, surprised to hear Borges talking this way. "Do you believe in God?" I asked him.

"Of course not," he smiled. "Though I remain a faithful Catholic."

I had to laugh. "How can that be?"

"Through another paradox, not half so clever as Zeno's," he replied. "I want the religion I don't believe in to believe in something."

I signaled to Diotima for another cup of coffee and another pot of maté for Borges. She smiled back at me, as beautiful as ever. I made a mental note to spirit her off to a tropical island and spend the rest of my life with her.

"You've been reading the newspaper, haven't you?" Borges said.

"Just the crime news," I lied. "A man was murdered and his body dumped in a cemetery."

"Is that news? What could be a better place for a corpse?"

"They should have buried him while they were at it. Set up a headstone: Here lies Stephen Albert."

Borges set his cup down with a clatter, his hand shaking. "What did you say? His name was Stephen Albert?"

"Yes. Stephen Albert, 36, of Medford. The body was found in Grove Street Cemetery, in Hyde Park."

"Is that near Medford?"

"No, not at all. Medford is north of Cambridge, Hyde Park is down near Dedham."

"Does the newspaper give his occupation?"

"High school biology teacher. What's the matter? Did you know him?"

Borges's face was pale. "I used that name in a story once. Stephen Albert. As the name of a man who was murdered solely on account of his name."

"On account of his name?"

"To send a message to another person."

"It's just a coincidence, I'm sure. How long ago did you write that story?"

"It must have been almost thirty years ago."

"Well, don't worry about it. This Stephen Albert was only six years old when you wrote that story."

Diotima glided up with our coffee and maté. Then she pulled a white envelope out of her apron pocket. "I almost forgot to give you this," she said. "I think it's for the gentleman here. It was stuck in the door when we got here this morning." She handed me an envelope addressed to "Sr. Borges."

"What is it?" Borges demanded.

"It's an envelope addressed to you."

"Open it. Is there a letter inside?"

"Just a handwritten note. Hand printed, actually."

Borges's forehead glistened with sweat. "Read it to me."

"*Achilles and Albert have met their doom,*" I read. "*In the name of God there will be more. It is written.*"

"In the name of God!" he repeated. "Is the note signed?"

"I guess you could say that. At the bottom it says, 'The Tortoise.'"

He buried his face in his hands and moaned softly for a minute or two. When he lowered his hands to face me again, it was with an intense, imploring expression, as if he was struggling to connect with me through the yellow haze. "What have I done?"

"Is something the matter?"

He scowled at my obtuseness. "First the marathon runner—"

"Achille Toulou?"

"Yes. Achilles. Then Stephen Albert—and now this note. I am the common thread."

"But Toulou wasn't even murdered. He was just running along Concord Avenue—"

"Don't you see?" Borges cried. "I am the cause of these deaths."

Within an hour we stood at the intake desk of the nearest Boston police station, the Back Bay district station on Harrison Avenue, being ignored by a paunchy Irish cop who seemed annoyed that we'd interrupted his afternoon nap. Borges insisted on doing the talking. When he mentioned Stephen Albert, the officer pushed a buzzer and we soon found ourselves in an interrogation room staring across a metal table at a plainclothes detective named Ed Harrity. Harrity was about fifty, with a gaunt face and thinning red hair. He had the air of a man who'd seen everything, any number of times, and refused to be impressed. He kept one of his faded blue eyes on the two-way mirror that occupied one of the walls. When he reached out to shake hands, he realized Borges was blind and turned to me. "You've got some information on Stephen Albert?"

"Yes," Borges answered. "And on the man they called Achilles."

"The runner? He was hit by a drunk driver, a guy named Colavito. Are you saying Colavito killed Albert too?"

"Not necessarily."

"Did he even know Albert?"

"Not as far as I know."

Harrity rolled his eyes. "Did you know either of them?"

"No, I didn't."

"Then what's the connection? If you don't mind my asking?"

"I am the connection."

"You?"

Borges nodded solemnly. "Let me explain. Almost thirty years ago I wrote a story in which I used 'Stephen Albert' as the name of a man who was murdered simply because of his name."

"A story?"

"And around the same time I wrote another story in which four murders took place, one at each of the four points of the compass, and at the end of that story—"

"Wait a minute! You're saying 'stories'—you mean stories, like short stories? Fiction?"

"Fictions, yes. But not any less true on that account."

Harrity glanced knowingly at the two-way mirror. "Mr. Borges," he said, "we appreciate your taking the time to come down here today. We're very busy, as I'm sure you know, so if you'll excuse me—"

"You don't understand!" Borges objected, fumbling in his jacket pocket.

"Of course things aren't always what they seem." The detective smiled as he edged toward the door. "Sometimes people see connections between events, random events, that aren't really there—"

"You don't understand!" Borges held out the note we'd been handed in the coffee shop. "I have a note from the Tortoise!"

For the briefest of moments Harrity seemed nonplussed, as if all his sang froid had been drained out of him. Then—possibly for the benefit of whoever was watching through the two-way mirror—he let out a loud, theatrical laugh. "What a coincidence! I just got a wire from the Tooth Fairy!"

He ducked into the hall and beckoned at me to follow him. "Now," he said in an unfriendly voice, "if you could escort your Dad back to the front desk."

"He's not my Dad," I said. "He's a famous Argentine poet—"

"Whatever he is," the detective growled, "I'll give you two minutes to get him the hell out of here!"

That rebuff by Detective Harrity gave Borges the inspiration he needed to launch his own investigation. "The police are idiots!" he growled as we drove back to Cambridge. "How can they solve these crimes if they won't acknowledge the connection between them?"

"Are you sure they're related? Maybe the runner's death—"

"You've read the note. They were death sentences carried out in the name of divine justice. How can they not be related?"

The Galaxie lumbered over the Mass Avenue bridge to Cambridge. I glanced over my shoulder—Borges always sat in the back seat—and saw him steadying himself with his walking stick as we swerved north on Memorial Drive.

"You will recall my lecture at Ipswich University that led to the capture of Mr. Jensen," he said. "For justice to be served, some person other than the killer and his victim must be aware of the crime and the killer's justification for committing it.   That person is the detective.   He is as essential to the crime as the murderer and his victim."

"But the crime would have been committed whether the detective knew about it or not."

"Nonsense!" Borges thumped the floor of the car with his walking stick. "I am that person. I am the detective."

For the next few days Borges was more excited than I'd ever seen him before.   He threw himself into his role as detective with a flurry of activity, most of which—the actual activity, that is—was left to me.   After all, I had the car; I could walk and I could see.   Other than the driving and the legwork—and the examination of evidence, clues and suspects, which was also my responsibility—he was perfectly capable of conducting an investigation.   He provided what he called ratiocination.

First we visited the site of Achille Toulou's death, where admirers had erected a small shrine in his honor, and we talked to Ben Colavito, the hapless drunk who killed him.   Colavito was out on bail, seemingly remorseful and depressed about what he had done.   He was a weak-chinned little man who hardly seemed capable of committing a crime worthy of being solved by Borges.   He didn't blink when we quizzed him about Stephen Albert, claiming never to have heard of the biology teacher.   On further questioning we learned that he lived about two blocks from Albert's house and his daughter attended the school where Albert taught— and he had been released on bail the day before Albert was killed.   "So what of it?" he whined, as if protesting some unjust amendment to the laws of chance.   "Can't there be coincidences anymore?"

"No," Borges replied. "There are no coincidences. Everything happens because it has to happen."

Albert's death remained an enigma. He left his school at the usual time and stopped at a convenience store at 4:00 p.m. When his car was found two days later—a dozen miles west of the city—its seats were stained with blood that matched his type. Evidently he'd been bludgeoned to death in his car and then dumped in the cemetery, where he was found with a hundred dollars in his wallet. The time of death was estimated at between 6:00 and 8:00 p.m. the previous evening.

"What time was the marathon runner killed?" Borges asked me.

"It must have been at about the same time. The newspaper described it as 'after dusk.'"

"What day was that? March 6?"

"I think so."

"And Stephen Albert died eight days later, on March 14—at the same hour."

"As far as we know."

"And the murderer dumped his body in the cemetery. Is that near where Achille Toulou was killed?"

"No, not at all. It's a good ten or twelve miles south of there."

"Tomorrow we're going to pay a visit to that cemetery."

I had never seen Borges happier or more engaged. He was in his element—gathering the facts, subjecting them to painstaking analysis, leaving no stone unturned. I think he would have been quite content to let the investigation go on forever.

And then disaster struck. In the affluent suburb of Brookline, a twelve-year-old girl named Mary Talbot was playing with her dog in her back yard—it was 7:00 p.m. on a

Monday evening—when she was hit in the right eye by an arrow. The arrow entered her brain and she died instantly. No one saw the shooter—whom the *Record-American* insisted on calling the "archer"—or any sign of unusual activity. Was it an accident? A reckless shot by some neighborhood kid playing cowboys and Indians? All the surrounding families were questioned; it appeared that none of them even owned an archery set. The police revealed that the arrow had been of the steel-tipped variety that is used for hunting elk and other large game; then they discovered a sort of shooting blind in the bushes behind the Talbot house, where the "archer" had apparently set up the shot and waited for his prey to step into range. The shocking conclusion was that the death of Mary Talbot had been a case of premeditated murder.

Thus began for Borges what he later called his dark night of the soul. Unaccountably, he blamed himself for the tragedy. He refused to eat or sleep, but sat in his darkened study, lost in a labyrinth of regret, shunning even the golden haze that might have led him to safety if he'd allowed anyone to raise the curtains. After a sleepless night his wife called and I rushed over to find the pair in the dining room, swooning in an atmosphere of frenzied but motionless activity. Borges, in his customary suit and tie, sat bent forward in an armchair next to the huge mahogany table—it could accommodate a party of eight—that came with the apartment; the table was piled high with books of poetry, philosophy, mysticism, even mathematics, in a dozen languages. From one of them Señora Borges stood reading aloud with her last breath of wakefulness as Borges nodded with his head in his hands, his cane propped between his knees. A buzzing fly circled the table and landed on his forehead, and he didn't flick it off. "Zeno was wrong," he said when I sat down beside him. "The arrow does reach its target. Swiftly, lethally—and irretrievably. Poor Mary Talbot! I should have seen it coming."

With a careless gesture he flicked the fly off his forehead. It buzzed around frantically, then landed on the table. "We spend our lives in a race against death, and as long as we live we think we're winning. Death is gaining on us, racing closer each day but never quite catching up, like Achilles in the paradox. And we're like the tortoise, lumbering forward stupidly, ignorant of the fate rushing up behind us simply because we're still alive. In his heart, every man secretly believes he can outrace death."

Suddenly Borges whipped his cane through the air and brought it down on the table with a whack that rang through the apartment like a gunshot. The fly, which he must have been able to locate by some sort of bat-like radar, lay squashed on the end of his cane.

"That belief is false," he said as if nothing had happened. "But for each of us, in our lifetime, it's a fallacy that can't be refuted."

I left Borges huddled among his books in that shadowy room, his wife tottering beside him in her long black dress, and walked down to Harvard Square to find some breakfast. I couldn't persuade them to interrupt their researches for food or rest—they were just starting on Plato's *Parmenides* when I left—and I half expected, on my return, to find them sprawled unconscious on the floor. Instead Borges greeted me with a gleam of triumph in his sightless eyes.

"The marathon runner was killed at dusk on the sixth of March," he said excitedly. "Stephen Albert died at the same time eight days later. And four days after that, at the same hour, Mary Talbot was killed by the arrow." He took a deep breath and exhaled slowly. "The next death will occur tomorrow night at precisely 7:00 p.m. And so on."

Those last three words were the most chilling. *"And so on?"*

"There will be more deaths—potentially a limitless number—until the series is brought to an end."

"But we don't know who the next victim will be, or where that person will be killed."

"Bring me a map of Boston. A detailed map that shows the whole city from north to south, east to west. My wife will supply the pins and thread."

"Pins and thread?"

"Just get the map, please!"

I ran back down to Harvard Square and bought a large folding map of Boston and took it back to the apartment. It was as if no time had elapsed while I was gone: Borges sat in his armchair beside the mahogany table, his wife stood beside him like a sleepwalker, holding in her outstretched hands a spool of black thread and four stick-pins of the type commonly used on bulletin boards.

"Now," he said, "spread the map out on the table and insert pins at the points where the first two deaths occurred."

"Stick them right into the table?"

"Stick them in! We haven't a minute to waste!"

I could hardly bring myself to damage the fine old mahogany table. "We don't know where Stephen Albert's death occurred," I hesitated.

"Stick a pin in where they found his body."

Señora Borges, holding out the pins, glared at me with the mad intensity of a Lady Macbeth. I had no choice but to obey. I spread out the map and gently placed one pin on Concord Avenue in North Cambridge and another on Grove Street Cemetery in Hyde Park.

"Now stretch your thread between those two points. Find the midpoint and set another pin in there. Where did you put it?"

My hand shook as the third pin found its target on Lee Street in Brookline.

Borges covered his face with his hands. "It's the home of Mary Talbot, isn't it? I'll never forgive myself for not seeing that in time. If I hadn't been so full of myself, it would have been obvious."

"Now what?" I asked, my voice shaking.

"Now insert your last two pins at the points that lie exactly halfway between that midpoint—the home of Mary Talbot—and the end points where Achille Toulou and Stephen Albert met their deaths."

Again I did as he asked.

"Where did you put them?"

"The first one," I said, "appears to be in the middle of the Massachusetts Turnpike. The other one, between Mary Talbot's house and Grove Street Cemetery, is in the middle of a church. Holy Name Church in West Roxbury."

"Ah." Borges sat quietly for a long time. Then he hoisted himself to his feet and extended his hand. "Thank you. My investigation is over."

"What do you mean?"

"As the mathematicians say, the proof is trivial."

"But what about stopping the murders? You said—"

"My investigation is over," he insisted. "And so is my stay in the United States. Señora Borges and I fly back to Buenos Aires tomorrow night."

I couldn't believe what I was hearing. "But your seminars, your lectures, your commitments at the university?"

He waved his hand dismissively. "They can do without another doddering old man. They've got plenty of them."

The next twenty-four hours saw a whirlwind of activity, in which I was only slightly involved, as Borges spent most of his time on the telephone making travel arrangements and settling his affairs. With no help from me, he booked a flight to Buenos Aires on Wednesday night at ten.

That morning he took a call from Ronaldo Pérez, the president of the Ibero-American Society, who insisted on taking him and his wife to lunch at a posh restaurant in downtown Boston. I tagged along as the driver and seeing-eye dog.

It was the kind of restaurant most people never see the inside of unless they work there. Widely spaced tables, linen tablecloths, silverware so heavy it bends your wrist and waiters who bestow their attentions like the last members of a once-powerful elite. On one end of the dining room—the end to which the *maître d'* escorted us at the Borges' torturous pace—a discreet bar was tucked into the corner. We navigated past quartets of elegant old ladies, whispering couples and a tableful of businessmen who sounded like they might have been from Texas. And when we finally reached our table I was unnerved to discover, watching from the bar not more than ten feet away, the jealous husband who'd shouted curses at Borges at the reception. The Argentine wine merchant, Hector Alarcón.

Pérez himself seemed unusually deferential, almost obsequious. For over an hour he praised Borges's work and exchanged archaic social niceties with Señora Borges. Then finally—as the waiter grudgingly served our dessert and coffee—he came to the point. "I invited you to lunch to make amends for what happened at the reception last week," he said. "I'm terribly embarrassed about that and I hope you'll forgive any discomfort it may have caused."

"Nothing happened that requires an apology," Borges said.

Alarcón swiveled on his barstool, apparently so he could hear our conversation. Borges, of course, had no way of knowing he was there.

Pérez kept his eyes on Borges. "Hector Alarcón is a proud man, as you can imagine. He has never apologized for anything in his life."

"Nor have I," Borges said.

"It's simply not in his nature as a Latin American to apologize"—Pérez gestured disdainfully toward the Texans at the next table—"as these shameless and hypocritical Anglo-Saxons are prone to do whenever they find it to their advantage."

Borges suppressed a smile. In Argentina he had often been accused of having Anglo-Saxon sympathies. In fact he had once visited Texas and enjoyed it very much.

"However," Pérez went on, "Señor Alarcón has authorized me to say that he regrets the incident, as does his wife, and he asked me to assure you that it will be without consequences, and that all parties, accordingly, will be expected to continue in the future as they have been in the past."

That was an odd way to phrase an apology. I glanced at Alarcón, who looked about as apologetic as a hawk getting ready to swoop down on its next meal. He paid no attention to me.

"And as for myself," Pérez said, "I was perhaps guilty of annoying you about that needlessly insulting review you wrote of my book. I continue to believe in the justice of my position and I reiterate my request for a retraction. But of course no apology is necessary for something that happened so long ago. You probably don't even remember what you wrote."

"I remember every word of it," Borges replied, "and if you wish, I could provide a line-by-line justification that would convince even a fool, and possibly yourself, that what I wrote was beyond dispute. But I couldn't retract it if I wanted to—time unfortunately proceeds only in one direction—and as you say, no apology is necessary."

"Very well," Pérez said, blushing. He turned around and signaled—in the Latin American style, by pretending to scribble on his palm—for the check.

"And now I hope you'll excuse us," Borges said, pushing himself into a standing position with his walking stick. "Señora Borges and I have much to do before we leave. We're booked on a ten o'clock flight to Buenos Aires."

"Is there anything I can do?" Pérez asked, lurching to his feet. "I'll send a driver to your apartment."

"This young man has graciously offered to drive us to the airport." Borges turned to me: "I meant to tell you," he said, "there's an errand I need to run before we fly out—it shouldn't take more than an hour. So please pick me up at exactly 6:15. We'll be back in plenty of time to pick up Señora Borges and our luggage en route to the airport."

As Borges and his wife began their arduous exit, I noticed another familiar face at the bar. Next to Alarcón, with his back turned, sat Isidro Pla, the quixotic Cuban who'd confronted Borges at the reception with bizarre charges of plagiarism. Pérez had offered no apology on Pla's behalf, and I wondered if he knew Pla was there. It wasn't even clear that Alarcón knew who he was.

Outside, I held my umbrella over the heads of Borges and his wife. It was the first day of spring and Boston was drenched in a bone-chilling rain. As he said good-bye, Pérez shook Borges's hand, which Borges detested. *"Buén viaje!"*

In the car, Borges sat quietly for a few minutes, then asked: "Hector Alarcón was sitting at the bar, wasn't he?"

"How did you know that?"

"I have ears. I could tell that Pérez was performing for an audience. And now, as it happens, they all know my schedule for this evening."

The Galaxie sailed across the bridge into Cambridge, wipers flapping desperately against the rain. "Sometimes I wonder if I've chosen to visit the wrong part of your wonderful country," Borges said. "Aren't there places where an old man can spend the winter without freezing to death? And wouldn't the madman in Oklahoma who thinks I stole his soul be preferable to this pack of lunatics in Boston?"

I picked Borges up promptly at 6:15, hoping it wouldn't be a long drive. Visibility in the Galaxie, between the rain and the fading daylight, had a half-life of about two minutes. "Welcome to springtime in Boston," I said. "Where are we going?"

"Drive south."

I crossed the Larz Anderson Bridge and proceeded south toward Cambridge Street.

"The fact that this is the first day of spring is important," Borges said, "though possibly not for the reason you suppose. The equinoxes, unlike the solstices, are human conventions—artificial lines drawn half way between the winter and summer solstices. Taken together with the solstices they divide the year into four parts, but that number could just as easily be eight or sixteen or infinity."

"In which case," I laughed, "you'd never catch your flight, would you? By the way, where are we going?"

"South, I told you. Is anyone following us?"

The rear-view mirror afforded an excellent view of the fogged rear window. The side mirror was hopelessly speckled with rain. "I can't see anything behind me."

"I didn't think so," he said. "What about the four cardinal points of the compass?"—I assumed it was a rhetorical question, posed to no one in particular or at least not to me; I just wanted to know where I was supposed to be driving—"North, south, east, west. You might think they correspond to the dimensionality of space. But that, the physicists tell us, is also a human convention, as arbitrary as the four seasons."

The Galaxie had ground to a halt at the bottom of a ramp leading up to the Massachusetts Turnpike, which at rush hour is the closest thing on earth to a black hole. I hoped that wasn't where we were going. "Now where?" I pleaded.

"Holy Name Church," he said.

"Wherever that is. I didn't bring the map."

"It's due south, exactly half way from Mary Talbot's house to Grove Street Cemetery."

"Why are we going there?"

"It's open for prayer until eight o'clock."

At the church, after I'd ushered him to the pew of his choice, Borges gave me explicit instructions. I was to stand outside in the driving rain while he took care of some business, presumably with the man upstairs (whose undivided attention he could count on, since the place was completely deserted). And then, in fifteen minutes—at exactly seven o'clock—I was to come back inside, no matter what happened in the meantime. Luckily there was an overhanging ledge to one side of the front steps where I could spend fifteen minutes asking myself what I had done to deserve this. Or so I thought. In fact what happened was that after about five minutes I was joined under the overhang by a man I'd never expected to see again: Detective Ed Harrity of the Boston Police, who'd given us an unceremonious sendoff from the district station less than a week before. Two uniformed cops stood in the rain awaiting further orders.

"My instructions are to go in at exactly seven o'clock," Harrity said, puffing on a cigarette. "Very strict."

"Same here," I said.

"All right, then. Let's wait."

At exactly seven o'clock the four of us mounted the steps and entered the church in time to witness a sight I'll never forget. Three feet in front of Borges stood a tall man wearing a feathered head-dress and aiming a revolver at

Borges's head. He was a white man but he was dressed like an Indian, muttering incomprehensibly in a sing-song voice.

Suddenly, without warning or hesitation, Borges swung his cane at the man's face, whacking him right between the eyes with a loud crack. The man shrieked and doubled over with his hands covering his bloody face, as the two cops ran forward, threw him to the floor and tied him up like a rodeo calf. It was all over in about five seconds.

"Are you all right, sir?" Harrity asked Borges.

Borges hadn't flinched while all this was going on. "Detective Harrity," he smiled, recognizing the police officer's voice. "I'd like you to meet an old friend of mine— Mr. James DeMarce, of Ponca City, Oklahoma."

More police arrived, then an ambulance and a TV news crew. Harrity asked Borges a lot of questions and received answers ranging from the cryptic to the nonsensical.

"Do you know why he was trying to kill you?"

"He thinks I stole his soul," Borges said. "An understandable reaction, don't you agree?"

Harrity glanced at DeMarce, strapped to a gurney and spouting obscenities as the EMTs worked on his broken nose. If I hadn't grabbed Borges's elbow and led him away, he might have found himself in the same ambulance as DeMarce.

"We'll need to see you at the station tomorrow morning."

"Certainly," Borges said. "I'll be there at ten."

Inching down the front steps, I tried to bring Borges back to reality. "By ten o'clock tomorrow morning, you'll be in Buenos Aires. We've got to hurry—your flight leaves in an hour."

"There isn't any flight to Buenos Aires," he laughed. "That was a ruse."

"You mean you knew all this was going to happen?"

"Of course."

I led him through the rain and fog to my car, which I'd parked a block away. For Borges, this was like a journey to the antipodes. He held his walking stick in one hand, the crook of my elbow in the other. The ambulance sped past us, lights flashing, as if the insanity of James DeMarce needed urgent attention. Borges didn't blink at the flashing lights, though his grip tightened when the siren howled beside us. The night multiplied endlessly in the puddles that flooded the street.

"Why was the solution so obvious?" I asked him.

"I knew the what, the when and the where, but not the *who*. At least not who the murderer was. As soon as I got that note, I should have known who the ultimate victim would be."

"But how did you—"

"Colavito wasn't worthy of suspicion in such a crime. The killer had to be a person of intelligence and imagination—an artist, if you will—who could conceive these murders as a unified whole and carry them out with the materials at hand. He read about Achilles's death in the news and saw his opportunity. In the phone book he found a Stephen Albert who lived near the scene of the accident in North Cambridge; he bludgeoned the poor man to death and dumped his body at the extreme southern end of the city. Thus he laid down the axis of the straight-line labyrinth in which he meant to trap his prey."

I started to ask a question but Borges stabbed his walking stick next to my foot, possibly to remind me of the fate of James DeMarce. "He knew the death of Stephen Albert would send a message, just as the death of the fictional Stephen Albert did in the story. That message could have been meant only for me. When I saw the note I knew the killer had to be one of my most diligent readers. But it was another story that led me to the solution. That was the story about the four murders corresponding to the points of the compass."

He stopped and aimed his sightless gaze into my eyes. If a blind man's eyes can express emotion, I saw sadness there, and guilt, and a twinge of self-revulsion. "Time is a web of paths that branch into an infinity of possible futures," he said. "When I wrote that story I was choosing, without being aware of it, to be here tonight, standing in the rain outside this parish church in West Roxbury, Massachusetts—a place I had never dreamed of being, in a future I never dreamed would occur—while an ambulance carries James DeMarce away to a lunatic asylum."

"I don't know how you could have—"

"I could have written a different story, or written that story in a different way. But that's the one I wrote and I had no choice but to live the consequences of my choice. Regrettably—again without knowing it—I was also choosing the fates of Stephen Albert and Mary Talbot, two young people whose lives were of infinitely greater value than my own."

We trudged silently to a corner and waited for the light to change. The fog parted as we stumbled out, but at the pace we were going I wondered if we'd ever get across the intersection. "Once the die had been cast," Borges said, "there was little I could do to save those young people. As for myself, I was almost undone by my own vanity. The murder of Stephen Albert following so close on the death of Achilles should have woken me up. But no, when I received the note—supposedly from the Tortoise—and the police wouldn't listen to me, I thought I was destined to play the detective: the seeker after truth, the bringer of justice; in short, to be the hero of the story. That self-regarding fantasy led to catastrophe. Soon afterwards came the third murder—poor Mary Talbot, pierced through the eye by an arrow that didn't stop in mid-air as Zeno's paradox predicted. No, the arrow that killed Mary Talbot hurtled across the infinite subdivisions of time and space and found its target without impediment, logical or otherwise.

"I was devastated. Not that I hadn't known an arrow can kill someone—Achilles himself was felled by an arrow. But Mary Talbot's death was not only real, it was my fault. It was the poisonous fruit of my own original sin: a lifetime of toying with ideas I didn't really understand, ideas I thought were merely philosophical or literary—ideas like infinity, eternity and multiplicity, as represented in paradoxes, archetypes and labyrinths—when in fact those ideas are real and they can kill people. It seemed to me that this was a sin for which there could be no redemption. During a long, sleepless night—or was it a whole week of them?—I wandered in the most fearsome labyrinth of all, the labyrinth of depression and regret. Not just an unpleasant psychological state but a realization that my whole intellectual life for almost seventy years had been based on a monstrous error, a quixotic indulgence that had now cost the lives of two innocent people."

"I'll never forget the way you looked when I arrived that morning," I said, "sitting there surrounded by your books, all the life drained—"

"Without my paradoxes," he cut me off, tottering as he gestured with his stick, "I was thrown back upon fatalism and despair, which is where my intellectual odyssey began many years ago, before I started writing. The world, I admitted to myself, is a monstrous machine, indifferent to human life, and there's nothing that can save us from our fates. And yet the more I brooded over questions I knew had no answers, the more I found myself searching for those answers in the same familiar places, the same conundrums where people from time immemorial have struggled to make sense of things that are beyond our understanding. I made my wife read to me all night, sometimes in languages she didn't understand. We read Schopenhauer, William James, and once again, Plato and the paradoxes of Zeno. And that was where I found the answer. Suddenly I glimpsed the reality that had been eluding me. It was in plain view, as the solution always is, right where it had been all along. The maze that is a single line, where more philosophers have lost themselves than in any other."

The rain had started again, slowing us down even more as I hobbled along balancing my umbrella over the old man's bald head. I could see the Galaxie glimmering under a street light, just beyond our reach. "I asked you to bring me the map of Boston," Borges went on, undaunted, "I asked you to mark out the sites of the first three deaths. And when you told me that the killing of Mary Talbot had occurred exactly at the midpoint between the deaths of Achille Toulou and Stephen Albert, I knew that the next crime would be committed in one of two places, each exactly half way between the place where Mary Talbot died and the two original murder sites. Which one would it be? You gave me the answer yourself when you found Holy Name parish on the map. The Holy Name: the Name of God. Don't you remember the note? 'Achilles and Albert have met their doom. In the name of God there will be more.' The fourth and last murder, I realized, would take place in that church.   And the timing was laid out in the same proportions, slicing each earlier interval in half: the second death eight days after the first one, the third death four days after that, and the fourth one two days later— tonight, March 20—at exactly 7:00 p.m. like all the others. And that death was meant to be mine."

"But what made you realize that?"

Borges stopped and faced me: cold rain dripped over his clenched brow. "When I purged my vanity and embraced my fate, I suddenly saw the truth: that I was not Achilles, but the Tortoise. The pursued, not the pursuer. I wasn't the detective, a step behind the killer—I was his quarry. And he was close on my trail."

He stumbled forward, almost losing his balance. "But who was he, this murderer? He could have been Isidro Pla, the delusional Cuban who accused me of plagiarism, claiming to have written the story about the murders at the four points of the compass.   Or he could have been Ronaldo Pérez or the vicious Hector Alarcón—or both of them, leading me to a gruesome death and pinning the blame on Pla or some other fool. And oh yes, it could have been the madman from Oklahoma. He was the one with the strongest motive."

We had reached my car but Borges couldn't stop talking. He clutched my elbow, pulling me toward him as I tried to open the door. "I had to get behind my pursuer. I had to find the place where I was destined to meet my doom and get there first. And when I knew the where and the when—which was obvious as soon as you stuck those pins in the table—I had to leave my trail exposed, I had to announce where I was going in front of all the suspects, so that any one of them could find me in the right place at the right time. Of course—as I should have known—the real killer didn't need my directions. He had lured me into his trap. But I was ready for him."

Borges rode quietly in the back seat all the way to Cambridge. I concentrated on my driving, ducking the headlights, trying to ignore the rain beating like a cosmic storm on the metal-and-glass carapace that carried us through space. "I can't believe we were out in that," I said as we pulled up in front of his building.

"Twenty-five hundred years ago," Borges said, "Zeno led us into a hall of mirrors to teach us that we have dreamed the world and everything we see in it is an illusion. A wonderful but not quite perfect illusion, with a few cracks in the mirrors to make sure we know not to trust them. But where does the dream come from? Is it a fabrication of the will, fated to disappear when we do—or the work of an indivisible divinity that lives in each of us?"

"Which you don't believe in."

"Of course not."

∞

I have two selves: the one who feels pain and the one who doesn't. That one—the one who feels no pain—stands apart with his back to the wall, to all appearances as real as I am. He smiles when I smile, winks when I wink, combs his sparse hair with the same flourish (quite vain he is, always fiddling with his hair, trimming his eyebrows, picking at blemishes on his skin), but he feels nothing. As I'm shaving he studies me closely, and if I nick my face he grimaces and seems to bleed, just as I do, but I know it's all a sham: he feels nothing and regards himself, for that reason, as a superior being. I can almost hear his disdain: "That man standing there, that Nick Martin, is different from me. To the rest of the world we're the same man, but that's an illusion: I'm pure light, as quick and weightless as desire, timeless if not immortal; he's flesh and blood, heavy with pain and regret, a dying animal like any other. Yet I'm fastened to him, no matter how bad he makes me look. Even now his pain distorts my face, though all I feel is pity."

Which one is real and which the reflection, I wonder? Sometimes, briefly, when the pain and regret are unbearable, I become that figure in the mirror, who winces but never cries out. Is one of us an impostor? Which one?

My daughters represent the two sides of my double life, though neither understands it. Gracie is all flesh and feeling,

Ingrid all intellect and detachment, like my image in the mirror; they compete as if one could exist without the other. Nilsa, with her loving hands, is the only person who brings my two selves together. I confess I am falling in love with her. The other fellow—is he a little jealous?—smirks at me as I comb my hair.

This afternoon Tom drove me to the real estate management company, located on the fortieth floor of a downtown skyscraper. In the sumptuous office suite we were greeted by Ms. Sheila McCurdy, a friendly but flint-eyed woman of about forty who introduced herself as the property manager and immediately disclaimed all responsibility for managing the property. "All we do is collect the rent," she explained with a smile. "The landlord is responsible for the condition of the building. If you describe your problem, I'd be happy to bring it to his attention."

I had deeper concerns than either she or Tom could imagine. "Who is the landlord?" I asked her.

She seemed unnerved by my question. "I'm not at liberty to disclose that information."

"But there is one?"

"One what? A landlord?" she laughed. "Of course there's a landlord!"

"Have you ever met him?"

"Not personally, but—"

"Have you ever talked to him?"

"Not personally." She turned away from me to face Tom. "Now what seems to be the problem?"

"There's a broken pipe under the sink leaking raw sewage into the kitchen," Tom said.

"You should look at your lease.   It says minor repairs are the tenant's responsibility."

"This is a major repair," Tom argued.   "Raw sewage—"

"From your point of view, perhaps."   Ms. McCurdy stood up and smiled, signaling that our meeting was over. "I'm sure the landlord is a very busy man with a lot on his mind.   He has more important things to do than worry about every leaky pipe."

"Will you talk to him about this?" Tom insisted.

"I'll do my best to bring your problem to his attention," she said, holding out her hand, "but I can't guarantee—assuming I'll be able to reach him—that he'll do anything about it."

I shook her hand. "So what should I do, then? Pray?"

"That's always a good idea," she said pleasantly.

It always puzzled me why Borges was so terrified of mirrors. He claimed to detest them on philosophical grounds, because they fill the world with abstractions. "A mirror creates an illusion which, being outside of time and space, is more terrifying than anything it reflects," he told me once. "A blind man can still see his nightmares."

Then one morning in the coffee shop I realized that what he saw in every mirror was a messenger of death. "All art and wisdom begin in the confrontation of two selves," he said as he stirred his maté. "The accidental, temporal self that clings to a dying body, and the archetypal self that underlies our experience and so can never be part of it.

That second self—the true self, if you credit the mystics—appears only at the moment of death, usually in a mirror."

"In a mirror?" I repeated.

"According to folklore," he smiled.

"Can everyone see it there?"

"Only the person who is dying.   To anyone else it would seem an illusion."

Our next case led us deep into the world of illusion, complete with magic carpets, sleight of hand and fantastic legal fictions.   It was a world like a magician's chest, constructed with so many baffles and reflections that no one could see through it, even a murder victim in those last, astonishing moments before death captured his image for the last time.   In such a world, is there anyone who can tell where illusion ends and reality begins?   *Only the person who is dying.*   To anyone else, even murder can seem like an illusion.

4.

Illusionists

> To make something true consists thus in giving the complete illusion of truth, following the ordinary logic of the facts and not merely transcribing them as they come tumbling along. I conclude that the most gifted Realists should instead be called Illusionists.
>
> Guy de Maupassant,
> Preface to *Pierre et Jean.*

Of all the conversations I had with Borges in that coffee shop, there were only a few that touched on his writing. We talked of world literature, philosophy and crime, particularly the cases we were working on. But it was rare for Borges to mention the subject he was most famous for: the writing of fiction. One such occasion stands out in my mind. It came near the end of his stay in Cambridge, and I hoped that, before he disappeared across the equator, he might impart a few secrets that would compensate me for the countless hours I'd spent as his chauffeur, guide, and all-purpose sounding board. Of course I'd been much more than that—or less, depending on how you look at it. I'd played Watson to his Holmes, Sancho Panza to his Don Quixote, Dante to his Virgil, Stephen Daedalus to his Leopold Bloom. That list—

as I was soon to learn—did not exhaust the possibilities. How could I have guessed that he fancied himself the avatar of an eighth-century Caliph of Baghdad?

"There are two kinds of fiction," he said as he sipped his maté. "Fantasy and realism, which in practice amount to the same thing. In fantasy, you imagine a reality different from the one you suppose actually exists, and you try to create the illusion that it's true; in realism you imagine the reality that you suppose actually exists, and you try to create the illusion that it's true. The first is difficult, the second all but impossible. In each case your aim is a perfect illusion of the truth, not the truth itself, which, especially in the case of the reality that actually exists, is a bewildering jumble of causes and effects, and probably unknowable. For this reason Maupassant said that realists—whether in art, literature or politics—should be called illusionists."

"Do you consider yourself a realist?" I asked him. "Or a fantasist?"

Borges chuckled indulgently. "If you write a realistic review of a book that was never written, you're called a fantasist," he said. "But if you write a novel about people talking in ways that people never talked and doing things that people never did, you may be complimented on your unflinching realism."

"What are you, then?" I laughed. "A realist or a fantasist?"

"An illusionist, of course. We're all illusionists."

A few days later he called with a surprise invitation. A Uruguayan friend had given him two tickets to an event he didn't want to miss. His wife was ill and unable to attend, he told me, and all his colleagues at Harvard were busy with departmental responsibilities. Would I be so kind as to accompany him to the Alhambra Theater in Boston on Friday night, where a famous troupe of illusionists (not the literary kind, of course) would give their last performance before embarking on a European tour? Naturally I agreed without a second thought. In the 1960s it was a commonplace—accepted by everyone from the lowliest college freshman to the entire population of France—that life was absurd. And so I found nothing extraordinary in being asked to escort a blind man to a magic show.

The Alhambra Theater was a baroque relic down by the docks, in a district of barricaded shops and looming brick warehouses. Borges wriggled out of the car and followed me down the cobblestone streets, clutching my elbow in one hand and his ivory-handled walking stick in the other. A cold moon squinted back at us from under scudding white clouds. We ducked through a pseudo-Moorish archway into the theater lobby, which had seen better days a lifetime ago. There we found chandeliers, faded wall hangings, oriental carpets—and a surprisingly elite crowd of men in tuxedos and women wearing jewels and evening gowns. Evidently this final performance was something of a social event. As we found our seats, Borges confessed his lifelong love of magic, kindled by Sir Richard Burton's translation of the *Arabian Nights* and by fortune tellers in Seville, *zarzuelas* in Madrid and *The Magic Flute* performed by marionettes in Geneva.

"I'm a little surprised that you'd want to be here," I said. "I mean... with your eyesight the way it is."

"My being blind, you mean."

"Right." That subject always made me uncomfortable. "You're not going to be able to see the stage."

"All the easier to avoid being deceived by appearances!" he laughed. He leaned toward me and whispered confidentially: "Let me know if anything unusual happens. For example, if a dove fails to fly out of a silk hat, or a lady remains whole instead of being sawed in half." In spite of his jokes he seemed anxious, bobbing his head uncomfortably, tugging at his collar, digging his fingernails into my arm at every unexpected noise.

The curtain rose and the magicians—two men and one woman—walked on stage and bowed to enthusiastic applause. "I've seen this show many times," Borges said. "Always with the same cast—in Geneva, Madrid, Buenos Aires, Montevideo. Like a film, it never varies in the least detail, no matter how many times you see it. I can probably give you a better description of it, moment by moment, than you could recite for me as you sit there watching it."

How could that be? I wondered. The magicians—he called them illusionists—looked far too young to have performed in front of Borges before he lost his sight. Admittedly they wore heavy makeup, flowing costumes and in the case of the male assistant, a mask; but a more likely explanation was that Borges's famous memory was playing tricks on him. Whatever the explanation, I soon realized that he meant to do exactly what he said he could do. As I watched the show, he described it to me, *sotto voce*, in every detail as it unfolded, as if I were the blind man and he the friend who'd come along to help me enjoy the performance.

The show was structured as a series of vignettes from the *Arabian Nights*, framed by the narration of Scheherazade. Scheherazade, as everyone knows, was a beautiful young woman who married a certain King Shahriyar in spite of his quaint practice (said to be a reaction to the infidelity of his first wife) of marrying a different virgin every night and chopping off her head in the morning. She hoped to wean him of this vice by entertaining him with a succession of stories that neared their dénouement with the first light of dawn. At morning's approach she would discreetly fall silent, leaving the poor king dangling in suspense—and he would spare her for one more night in order to hear the end of the story. This went on for a thousand and one nights, at which point Scheherazade apparently ran out of stories, and the kindly King Shahriyar spared her for the sake of the three sons she'd borne him in the meantime. In the magic show, each illusion appeared as the climax of one of Scheherazade's tales, performed by a cast of storybook characters: Harun al-Rashid, the magnificent Caliph of Baghdad; Jafar, his Vizier or chief counselor; Masrur, Chief Eunuch and Executioner; and an assortment of slave girls, virgins and queens, together with a few familiar faces such as Aladdin and Sinbad the Sailor. The troupe consisted of only three actors: The Great Abdul, master magician, playing King Shahriyar, the Caliph Harun al-Rashid, and sometimes the Vizier Jafar; Scheherazade, who narrated the tales and also played the slave girls, virgins and queens; and an assistant who, by changing masks, could switch between the identities of Aladdin, Sinbad, Jafar and Masrur as the occasion demanded. At every moment there was an undercurrent of sex, bondage and sadism, centering around the voluptuous Scheherazade and her impersonations. The Caliph Harun al-Rashid liked to disguise himself as a merchant and wander the streets of Baghdad in search of adventure, accompanied by the cringing Jafar, whom he constantly threatened with decapitation for some minor infraction. To accomplish this, he let it be known, he had merely to snap his fingers and Masrur the Executioner would appear carrying a sword and a blood-stained leather mat, upon which the victim, without being asked, would be expected to kneel, head bowed, hands behind his back.

After a few card tricks to warm up the crowd, the show opened with Scheherazade relating the history of the misogynistic king. Evidently he was inspired by his brother, Shah Zaman, who, on discovering his wife in bed with a slave, drew his sword and cut them both in half. This set the stage for the first illusion, "The Vengeance of Shah Zaman," which, not surprisingly, consisted of The Great Abdul sawing a lady in half (the lady being Scheherazade herself after a quick costume change behind a screen). Though a slower death than being slashed with a sword, being sawed in half proved a more merciful one, since the lady could still wiggle her arms and legs and even smile at the audience after being dismembered. The next two illusions—"The Genie of the Lamp" and "Badroulbadour's Magic Carpet Ride"—came from the story of Aladdin and his wonderful lamp. They involved clouds of black smoke, the disappearance of various objects, the levitation of Badroulbadour (Aladdin's love interest, played by Scheherazade in emerald harem pants) on a magic carpet, and even the transformation of a man (the masked assistant) into a dog. Borges described all this to me as it unfolded on the stage, paying scant heed to our neighbors in the audience who tried to quiet him. I think it was his anxiety that kept him talking. "Talking to save a life," he explained later. "As if I could stop time in its flight."

At intermission he insisted that we pick our way through the crowded aisles to the lobby, where several dozen well-heeled patrons of the arts were attempting to yak each other to death. They hovered in their tuxedos and evening gowns, fueled by cocktails and self-congratulation (the performance was a benefit for some unspecified charity, probably a mental hospital). Consistent with the program, there was a preponderance of charlatans, thieves, courtesans and eunuchs. Close beside us, guzzling a pair of martinis which he held in either hand, stood a burly, white-haired buffoon in evening dress, entertaining a small coterie of admirers with an interminable anecdote about a race horse. He reeked of alcohol and had an unmistakable air of corruption and incompetence. We later learned that he was the Chief of Police.

The lights flickered and we began the cautious ascent to our seats. As we walked, Borges fleshed out Scheherazade's narration with his own commentary on the *Arabian Nights* and its place in world literature.

"I confess I haven't read the *Arabian Nights*," I told him.

"Nobody has," he said. "If you try to read it, you'll be dead before you finish. The book is infinite."

The second half of the show featured "The Ebony Horse," which The Great Abdul sent flying over the orchestra pit, and an illusion called "The All-Seeing Eye of Prince Ali." Finally, after a portentous drum roll, Scheherazade announced that the time had arrived for the world-famous climax of the show, one of the most famous illusions in all of magic: "The Vizier's Decapitation" by Masrur the Executioner.

Caliph Harun al-Rashid, played by The Great Abdul, has fatally turned against Jafar, his Vizier or chief counselor. He snaps his fingers to summon the executioner Masrur, who appears in the person of the masked assistant, carrying his sword and the blood-stained leather mat. The Great Abdul disappears momentarily behind the screen and reappears in the robes of Jafar, who submits calmly to his fate. Masrur unrolls the leather mat in front of him and steps back, gripping the sword in both hands. Jafar kneels and bows his head, hands behind his back.

The suspense is unbearable, the room as quiet as death. Masrur's sword hovers over his head, then dives like a hawk, slicing through the Vizier's neck with a sucking sound. The illusion is perfect: The head drops and rolls away; the neck spurts blood, soaking the executioner's robe. The headless body crumbles on the leather mat. The executioner steps over the mat and disappears offstage. The leather mat glistens with blood.

The crowd holds its breath, unable to break the illusion. Scheherazade screams a bloody scream, gaping at the corpse. The curtain falls, sagging as it bounces on the stage.

A few hands clap but quickly stop. The audience—even Borges, who can't have seen anything—senses that something is wrong. And we all know what it is. The illusion was perfect, too perfect to be an illusion. This time what we saw was real.

The house lights flashed on and a terrifying disembodied voice ordered the audience to stay calm. Within minutes a dozen uniformed policemen appeared and began escorting the audience to the emergency exits. Borges insisted on being taken backstage. "I am Dr. Jorge Luis Borges," he told the officer at the end of our aisle, waving his cane as I held on to his elbow. "They are expecting me."

The officer stepped aside to let him pass but tried to block my way with his nightstick. "This young man, unfortunately, is blind," Borges said. "He must come with me."

We mounted the steps beside the stage and slipped behind the curtain, where we found the Chief of Police, still in evening dress and more than a little tipsy, attempting to exercise the powers of his office. He stood with his beefy arms folded across his even beefier chest, conferring with a Lieutenant McGarry, who wore the uniform of a plainclothes detective (rumpled gray suit, size 46 portly, over an unkempt white shirt, with a tie that reached only mid-way to his belt). A crowd of uniformed cops scurried around inspecting the scene of mayhem on the stage.

Scheherazade crouched on the floor, sobbing over the remains of The Great Abdul: a twisted, blood-soaked pile of Arabian robes, and some distance away, a head—the eyes captured in a goggle of eternal astonishment. When she saw Borges she jumped up and threw herself at his feet, babbling in some language I didn't understand. Evidently she and Borges knew each other from way back—and, as I was startled to realize, it must have been way, way back, for the lovely Scheherazade, beneath all her makeup and jewels, was at least fifty years old. She appeared not Arabian but Asian, possibly Chinese. "Jorge!"—she was the second person I'd heard call him Jorge—"I'm so glad you are here. My husband"—evidently The Great Abdul had been her husband—"has performed his last trick. His most audacious illusion, 'The Vizier's Decapitation,' has cost him his life." She began sobbing again. "What a fate! To be murdered on stage... in front of hundreds of people! I beg your help in solving this mystery!"

"There's no mystery about it," Lieutenant McGarry scoffed, stepping up beside us. "The entire audience—including the Chief of Police—saw the assistant, the man who was playing Masrur, chop your husband's head off."

"That's what they *think* they saw," Scheherazade said, her voice steadying as she rose to her feet. She peered past us into the wings, where policemen prowled with flashlights in search of clues.

"Why do you say that?" Borges asked her.

"There was something about Masrur in that last illusion that didn't seem right," she said. "Something in his movements, his gestures. As if it wasn't really Bruno beneath the mask."

"Bruno?"

"That's the assistant's name, Bruno Eissler. He's been with us for many years. How could he have done this?" She began to cry again.

"Don't worry, ma'am," Lieutenant McGarry said. "We'll find him."

"But didn't you say you thought it wasn't Bruno?" Borges asked.

"What I said," she sobbed, "was that in that last scene, when he was playing Masrur the Executioner, he didn't seem quite himself, he didn't seem to be moving the way he usually does. It was as if—"

Just then a pair of burly cops dragged a man out of the shadows, clapped him in handcuffs, and shoved him into the center of the stage, calling out to the lieutenant that they'd caught the killer. They found him hiding in a closet in his dressing room, they said, pretending to be asleep. He seemed groggy and confused, unsteady on his feet, as if he didn't know what he was doing there. But he wore the robes of Masrur, and Masrur's mask dangled on a string around his neck. There could be no doubt that he was the assistant who had killed The Great Abdul.

"What's your name?" Lieutenant McGarry demanded.

"Bruno Eissler," the man said with a European accent. "What's going on?"

"You know what's going on. You just killed The Great Abdul."

The Chief of Police stepped toward us and sneered at Bruno. He was now wearing his topcoat and had been joined by his wife, who seemed anxious to get on with her evening. With a quick gesture he pulled the lieutenant aside, as if to impart some secret information, and then said in a booming voice: "Listen, McGarry, we're leaving on a cruise on Wednesday and I want this case wrapped up before then. Ask the Medical Examiner to schedule the inquest for Tuesday. Do you understand? You have three days to solve this murder." He sliced an open hand across his throat and laughed uproariously. "Or else!"

Borges cleared up the first mystery as I drove him back to Cambridge. Our trip to the Alhambra Theater, he explained, had not been taken on a whim; it had nothing to do with Uruguayan friends, Harvard colleagues or his wife's health.

Three days earlier he'd received a note from Scheherazade—her real name, he told me, was Jade Gogol, but he always thought of her as Scheherazade—asking him for help. Her husband suspected that someone was trying to kill him, and he feared that the killer would strike in the midst of a performance, bringing infamy as well as death.

Borges had known Scheherazade for many years. He'd even loved her once, when they were both much younger. She was beautiful then, an enchantress who could charm a man with her unending supply of stories. "Now," he said, "she's something of a bore, a blabbermouth who doesn't know when to stop talking. Many years ago we spent an evening together at an elegant restaurant in Buenos Aires. Her husband was out of town and it promised to be a romantic evening. We sipped red wine and talked of many things: time as a river, the moon as metaphor, the prose of De Quincey and Stevenson. But gradually the conversation lapsed into a monologue. She went on and on with her endless stories; she couldn't stop talking, even when I tried to make love to her. The night wore on and finally I dozed off, more susceptible, for once in my life, to the wine than to the woman—I won't go into that. Except to say that the evening ended with a chaste kiss and we have remained good friends over the years. And so when she asked me for help I couldn't refuse."

"What did she expect you to do?"

"She enclosed a pair of tickets for that last performance and asked me to attend. Her husband—The Great Abdul— was convinced that the killer would strike then."

"But if he thought this Bruno Eissler was trying to kill him, why didn't he just throw him out of the show?"

"You assume Eissler is the murderer."

"I saw him do it. So did everyone else in the audience."

"Everyone but me," Borges smiled.

Scheherazade tapped on Borges's door the next night a little before ten o'clock. He seemed to be expecting her—perhaps that was why he'd invited me to stay for dinner and then offered to share an excellent bottle of port if I'd sit with him a little longer. Señora Borges had retired to her room, and thanks to the port, a warm glow of well-being had settled over the apartment. I stumbled to my feet and opened the door: Scheherazade breezed in before I realized who she was. She wore a stylish red dress under a black velvet cape, with net stockings and stiletto heels; painted eyebrows, false eyelashes, and an impasto of makeup did their best to conceal her age. As thin as a wasp, she flitted into the living room where Borges sat and hovered over him as he rose and offered her a seat. He'd had an exhausting day, fielding calls from reporters and detectives about the events at the Alhambra Theater, and I wondered if he'd have any patience left for his old flame. He smiled wearily in anticipation of the long night ahead.

"Bruno Eissler has been charged with my husband's murder," she said after a few preliminaries. "I fear it is a great injustice."

Borges said nothing. To fill the silence, I asked her: "How can that be? Isn't it obvious that Eissler—"

"There is so much to tell," she cut me off. "Tales within tales within tales. Every lie contains two truths, every truth two lies, and so on forever and a day. You know that only too well, Jorge. Where should I begin?"

"With the truth," I suggested.

She reached over and touched Borges's hand. "I'll never forget the night we dined together at the Alvear Palace in Buenos Aires. What year was that? Could it have been 1939? I was a different woman then—just a girl, really—and you were a different man. Funny how things have turned out, isn't it?"

Borges nodded and withdrew his hand. "Go on," he murmured sleepily. "Tell your story."

She settled back in her chair, letting her eyes drift upward as if she were summoning her memories from above. "Young as I was," she said, "I'd already been enslaved by The Great Abdul, as he insisted I call him even after our marriage. I'd been raised in San Francisco by strict Confucian parents, but my family had fallen on hard times, and as the youngest of six daughters I faced a life of degradation unless I could find some way to earn a living. I joined a Chinese circus and learned a few magic tricks, and to pass the time in my idle moments I made up stories to amuse the acrobats' children.

"One fateful day the man who later became known as The Great Abdul overheard me telling stories at the theater. He was on tour from Boston, where he'd taken over a traveling magic show after ousting the master magician who'd founded it and directed it for many years. His name was Leon Gogol, and he was Russian, not Arabian, which should not surprise you, since everything about the man was a fraud. He was a master of technique, yet lacked the slightest shred of creativity. He could perform his illusions flawlessly, but he couldn't begin to put a story around them. To imagine a narrative structure linking the tricks into a show was completely beyond his capabilities. For that he needed me. Perceiving a spark of creativity in my storytelling, he made me his virtual slave. He beat me, chained me in his dressing room, and threatened to sell me to a marriage broker or a brothel—such were the career prospects of a Chinese girl in San Francisco in those days— if I didn't come up with stories for his magic show. I found a collection called the *Arabian Nights* and suggested that he build his act from tales in that collection. Night after night I labored to satisfy his insatiable demand for new stories, knowing that my life would be over if my creativity flagged for even one night. I had to construct a series of scenes in the Arabian style to fit the illusions he had already mastered —disappearances, reappearances, magical transformations, and finally the dramatic climax, 'The Vizier's Decapitation.'

"My tormentor, styling himself The Great Abdul, renamed his show 'Abdul's Arabian Circus' and took it on tour to international acclaim. I remained in his captivity, enforced by his threat to abandon me in some benighted land where I would be subject to an even more degrading form of slavery. After almost three years I acceded to his threats and married him—an acquiescence he would regret to his dying day, for my imagination died with my marriage vows. After our wedding, I never came up with another idea for the show, and it hasn't changed for thirty years. That's why you, Jorge, could still envision the illusions unfolding on the stage, in spite of the many years that have passed since you watched them. But I fear that the show's invariability has been its undoing, as well as mine. Since the performance was so unvarying, it was easily imitated, down to the least word and gesture—and that, I believe, is what led to my husband's brutal death.

"I will admit that over the years my attitude toward The Great Abdul had softened, as his treatment of me improved. We were never a loving couple, but I discharged the duties of honor that a wife owes to her husband, and until a few weeks ago I believed that he had conducted himself honorably as well. Then, shortly after our arrival in Boston, I discovered that The Great Abdul, true to his character, had been deceiving me for many years. He had another wife. The woman's name is Janice Brown and she lives about twenty miles north of here, in a town called Concord. Evidently—"

"Concord!" Borges exclaimed, suddenly revived. He opened his eyes wide. "The city of Emerson and the Transcendentalists! The home of Thoreau, Hawthorne and the Alcotts—"

"Evidently," Scheherazade cut him off, "*La Brown* was as much a victim of my husband's deceit as I was. He never told her he was married, and she fell to the deception that he was an Arabian sheik. When she discovered that he was really a Russian illusionist named Leon Gogol—and more shockingly, that he was also a bigamist—she dug into his past for information she could use to destroy him. She found half a dozen other so-called wives in various cities; she located court records of arrests for forgery and counterfeiting in the years before he became famous; she searched out his former master—another Russian illusionist, named Ivan Morloff, who also pretended to be Arabian— and learned of the deceitful tactics he'd used to wrest control of the act from that unfortunate man. Then one afternoon while we were setting up our props she stormed into the theater, hurling accusations at The Great Abdul with the precision of a knife thrower. The ensuing scene can hardly be imagined, even by one steeped in the violent excesses of the *Arabian Nights*. 'I have just met Ivan

Morloff,' she told my husband, recounting a visit to his former boss. 'He despises you for what you did to him, and wishes you an early and excruciating death. He attends every one of your performances in anticipation of the inevitable day when you will make a fatal mistake and reveal yourself as a fraud and a charlatan.' The Great Abdul laughed in her face. 'Is that what you've come here to tell me?' 'No,' she said, 'I'm here to tell you that I know our marriage is one of your tricks. My whole life is an illusion, as yours will be soon. You have made a fatal mistake, and you will not live long to regret it.' By the time Janice Brown left the theater, I realized that she was a demon in human form, a she-tiger from another world with unimaginable resources of cunning and cruelty in her feline eyes. She's a muscular woman, similar in build to our assistant Bruno Eissler, and I believe—"

Borges's head had begun to bob up and down as he struggled to stay awake, and when Scheherazade noticed this she lowered her eyes and fell silent. After a dagger-like glance in my direction, she stood up, threw her cape around her shoulders, and bowed to Borges. "Pardon me!" she begged. "I've stayed far too late."

"Not at all," he said.

"In any case"—she pretended to glance at her watch— "I have an important engagement. Perhaps I could come back tomorrow?"

"Certainly."

"All right, then," she smiled. "Same time tomorrow."

* * *

The next night, after Señora Borges had retired to her room, Borges and I sat in our accustomed seats sipping port (on this occasion an excellent Ferreira supplied by one of his admirers in the Ibero-American Society), and again shortly before ten o'clock Scheherazade tapped on the door. Her outfit was even more extravagant than the night before—a yellow silk shawl over zebra-striped leotards and an ankle-length slit skirt—and she was festooned from head to toe with jangling pendants, bracelets and bangles, perhaps in the vain hope of keeping Borges awake. Borges nodded politely but showed no inclination to speak.

Scheherazade sat in the same chair as the night before, with her eyes cast down as if waiting for one of us to turn on the sound. "Where was I?" she sighed.

"You were telling us about The Great Abdul and his Arabian Circus," I said.

"Ah, yes!" Her eyes brightened. "The Great Abdul owed everything to me. An illusionist, you understand, must have an assistant who believes in his illusions even when no one else does. This is a role that typically falls to the wife, practiced as she is in conscious self-delusion. Her credulity must be palpable and sympathetic, so it can be mimicked by the audience. I played this role for thirty years and made The Great Abdul what he was. He too began as an assistant to a master illusionist—that man, as I mentioned last night, was named Ivan Morloff but he called himself The Great Abdullah. The similarity in stage names is no coincidence. My husband's strategy, after he'd mastered his craft, was to imitate The Great Abdullah, substitute for him, overshadow him and finally replace him, on the assumption that the public wouldn't notice the difference. This is exactly what happened. When I met him he'd just taken over the act. He mocked his former master and called him "Abdullah Who Couldn't Be Dullah." In fact Morloff was a shy, bookish man who shunned the spotlight, preferring to spend his time browsing in libraries or dining at his favorite restaurants. He had gradually receded from the limelight, allowing my husband to take over his public identity, until he realized too late that he'd been replaced. But my husband, as I've told you, was utterly lacking in imagination. Having become The Great Abdul, he was powerless without me to weave a convincing narrative around it. All this is just background, of course. Now where was I in the story?"

Borges leaned forward, surprisingly alert. "I believe you had started telling us about the other wife."

"Ah! The demon woman!" Scheherazade turned away and pretended to spit on the floor. "I believe—no, I'm absolutely certain—that she murdered The Great Abdul. When she learned the depth of his perfidy, she began to plot her revenge. She met with Ivan Morloff and questioned him about the illusions until she understood how they were carried out. Secretly she attended our performances every night, memorizing each of Bruno's movements and gestures. You'll recall that Bruno wore a mask and a costume of flowing Arabian robes. It was a simple matter for a woman of the same size and strength to imitate his every movement. On the night of the murder, she hid in Bruno's dressing room and stole up behind him during the intermission. She drugged him with chloroform, using just enough to render him unconscious for an hour without killing him, and dragged him into a closet. Then she put on his mask and one of his spare costumes and took his place on the stage. From Ivan Morloff she had learned the secret of 'The Vizier's Decapitation.' She knew that if she ignored the mirrored images seen by the audience she could strike off The Great Abdul's head and have her revenge."

Borges stared at her intently with his sightless eyes. "Have you discussed this theory with the police?"

"I spoke to Lieutenant McGarry this morning. I told him about the demon woman and her insane threats and the evil aura that surrounds her. And I told him what I told you the night of the murder: that Bruno's movements and gestures hadn't seemed quite right as we performed the last set of illusions. That's because it wasn't Bruno. The last thing Bruno remembers is sitting at his dressing table and being smothered by someone who surprised him from behind."

"He carried a strong smell of chloroform when they pulled him out of the closet," Borges said, leaning forward again. "I noticed that at the time."

"There's something else," she hurried on. "The lieutenant told me about a piece of evidence he regards as highly suggestive. Everyone saw the blood spurt from my husband's neck onto the assistant's robe. I saw it: the robe was literally soaked in blood. But the costume Bruno was wearing when the police found him in the closet was spotless."

"Spotless?"

"Yes, spotless! Which means that the person who killed my husband and escaped in the bloody costume was not Bruno Eissler but the demon woman who calls herself Janice Brown. As I told the lieutenant this morning—"

Borges was literally on the edge of his seat. When Scheherazade noticed that she had aroused his attention, she lowered her eyes and fell silent. "Oh, my!" she exclaimed, glancing at her watch. "Please forgive me, but I must go." She stood up quickly. "May I come back tomorrow night?"

Borges smiled graciously, though I could see the annoyance on his face. "Until tomorrow, then," he said. "I can't wait to hear the conclusion of your story."

She bowed and fluttered out the door. I had to admire her. Over the years many people had attempted to charm Borges, to impress him, to enlist his aid, to divert him from his purposes—all to no avail. Had he finally met his match? "I've got a feeling that her story still won't be finished when she leaves tomorrow night," I said.

He nodded grimly. "Sometimes I feel like chopping her head off anyway."

Borges spent the next morning attending to some personal business, or so he told me when he called after lunch and asked me to drive him downtown to see Lieutenant McGarry. I had nothing I needed to do—only a couple of classes and a meeting with my new advisor, who probably wanted to ask me why I never went to class. Nothing, in other words, that seemed as important as solving a high-profile murder case, even if the solution, as everyone agreed, was obvious. Did I say *everyone*? I should have said everyone but Scheherazade, from whom, I knew, we would be hearing more that evening.

With its windows open on a beautiful spring day, the Galaxie seemed to be flying into town. As usual, Borges sat in the back seat, steadying himself with his walking stick. "If we were in Buenos Aires," he said, "I would ask you to drive me to a shop called *El Centro Mágico de Fu Manchu*, located at the intersection of Riobamba and Bartolomé Mitre, to talk to my friend David Bamberger. David is the scion of an illustrious Dutch family of magicians. He opened the shop recently after performing successfully for many years as 'Fu Manchu,' a name which, for legal reasons, he could not use outside of South America. In adopting the name and identity of the diabolical Chinese mastermind, he followed the tradition of the famous Chung Ling Soo, an American named William Robinson who passed as Chinese for many years before he was killed onstage."

That last detail grabbed my attention. "Killed onstage?"

"By one of his assistants," Borges added. "They were enacting a scene from the Boxer Rebellion. An execution by firing squad, I believe."

"And the magician—this Chung Ling Soo—was an American pretending to be Chinese?"

Borges made a dismissive noise, half snort, half growl. He hated redundancy—it reminded him of mirrors and reproduction, both of which he regarded as abominations. I should have known better than to ask him a question he'd already answered. "For some illusionists," he said, "the first step is to impersonate a more exotic nationality. Americans and Englishmen claim to be Egyptian, Indian or Chinese, and we know of at least two Russians and one Chinese-American woman who pass themselves off as Arabians to satisfy the narrative they've woven around their illusions."

We crossed the bridge into Boston, a city of one-way streets that all run in the same direction, with the result that, like Zeno's arrow, you can never reach your destination. Borges would have appreciated the irony of this traffic pattern if he'd been aware of it; but blind as he was, and swaying unsteadily in the back seat, he probably assumed we were making progress as I whipped the car down one street after another in search of the police station, which was probably less than a block from where we'd crossed the river.

"You seem to be driving in circles," he said to my surprise. "Or are we back in that maze that consists of a single line?"

"It's worse than that," I admitted. "I have no idea where we're going."

"Well, please hurry up and get there."

I navigated a few more one-way streets—weaving in and out of lanes, racing through red lights, slamming on the brakes at stop signs—but none of this took us any closer to the police station. Borges had started thumping his walking stick on the floor, a sign of impatience, if not annoyance. If I were a magician, I thought, at least I could create the illusion of progress.

Borges must have read my mind. "To create a great illusion," he said, "whether in magic or any other art, you must first deceive in a hundred little ways. It's like putting on a play. You need a plot that has a beginning, a middle and an end, with the right balance of inevitability and surprise. Then you must draw the audience in with simulation, empathy, catharsis, and at last an offer of complicity—for no audience can be fooled unless it wants to be. In the hands of an artist, any audience, having paid the price of admission, will welcome the deception, even demand it as its right."

Suddenly the police station loomed beside us, an undistinguished brick building in the middle of a parking lot. I landed the Galaxie and found Borges smiling mischievously in the back seat.

"Why are we going to see Lieutenant McGarry?" I asked him.

"I want to give him something new to think about."

It took some doing to get Borges out of the car, into the building, and past the security desk to the cramped, smelly little room the police use for interviews. Lieutenant McGarry grudgingly consented to grant us two minutes of his time. I could see why the lieutenant's schedule was so tight and why he seemed so unreceptive. On Friday night the Chief of Police had given him three days to solve the murder, and now it was Monday afternoon, halfway through the third day. His boss had made it clear that heads would roll if the Medical Examiner couldn't make conclusive findings at the inquest scheduled for Tuesday. The last thing Lieutenant McGarry wanted was something new to think about.

"Dr. Borges would like to bring something to your attention," I told him. "He was an eyewitness to the murder."

The lieutenant glanced at Borges's cane and then into his clouded eyes. "Let me get this straight," he said. "You're an eyewitness?"

"That is correct."

"Excuse me if I'm wrong—but you're blind, right?"

"That is also correct. But I am also a poet, and as such—"

"What's that got to do with anything?"

"—I am a visionary, a seer, an eyewitness to things unseen."

Lieutenant McGarry rolled his eyes. "All right. What can I do for you?"

"There's something I think you should know about," Borges said. "In 1918, in London, a famous magician who called himself Chung Ling Soo died after having been shot in front of hundreds of spectators as he performed his most famous trick. This consisted of being shot at with a rifle and apparently catching the bullet in his hand. In reality—"

"In reality I don't have all day."

"This will only take a minute. In reality the bullet was supposed to remain in a dummy barrel while a blank cartridge was discharged, but on that particular occasion—"

"With all respect," the lieutenant interrupted, "The Great Abdul was killed with a sword, not a gun, and I can't see how something that happened fifty years ago could have any bearing on the case. Your two minutes is up." He turned and headed out the door, leaving us by ourselves in the cramped, smelly little room. Evidently this was our punishment for annoying the police.

"I had a bad dream last night, Lieutenant," Borges called after him. "I dreamed that I was you, and I'd been given three days to solve a murder or have my head chopped off."

Lieutenant McGarry stopped and peered back inside. "Did you solve it?"

"No, I'm afraid not. I allowed myself to be deceived by appearances."

"That's funny," the lieutenant smiled, still peering around the door jamb, "because I had a similar dream. I dreamed that I was a blind man and I couldn't even see the appearances. So I tried to solve the murder based on a story about something that happened fifty years ago. How's that for a dream? Now if you'll excuse me, I have work to do."

The journey home was even more arduous than our trip into the city. The traffic was thickening in the late afternoon sun, and none of the one-way streets led in the direction we needed to go. I was hoping Borges would tell me more about the death of Chung Ling Soo and explain what that distant event had to do with the murder of The Great Abdul. Instead he related a tale from the *Arabian Nights*. "I call it the story of the two dreamers," he said, "but Burton called it 'The Tale of the Ruined Man who became Rich Again through a Dream.' It is told that a young man of Baghdad, who had inherited great wealth, squandered it in thoughtless generosity. Then he dreamed that if he went to Cairo he would find his fortune and become rich again. He journeyed to Cairo and fell asleep in a mosque, and when a gang of robbers raided the house next door, he was mistakenly arrested, interrogated and beaten by the local Chief of Police. When he told the Chief of Police why he'd come to Cairo, the Chief of Police laughed and recounted a similarly foolish dream, in which he, the Chief of Police, had imagined himself finding buried treasure in a house in Baghdad, which he described in detail. The young man recognized the house as his own. He journeyed back to Baghdad and dug up the treasure and was a rich man again. The story, in Burton's translation, after customary homage to the power of Allah, characterizes these events as a marvelous coincidence."

I had to laugh. "A coincidence? That's a funny way to describe it."

"If you look at the world in a certain way," Borges said, "the probability that any one element in a chain of events will occur in conjunction with any other is so low that the whole chain of events seems like a marvelous coincidence. If the young man hadn't dreamed as he did, he would never have been arrested in Cairo. If he hadn't been arrested in Cairo, he would never have told his dream to the Chief of Police. And if the Chief of Police hadn't related a similar dream, the young man would never have found the treasure that lay waiting for him in his own garden."

"If you look at the world in a certain way," I said, "*everything* that happens is a coincidence."

"Indeed it is," Borges agreed. "Two mutually self-fulfilling dreams such as this story describes are like a pair of facing mirrors that reflect an infinite duplication of images back on themselves. Such a marvelous coincidence can occur only in an *Arabian Nights* world, where 'the pen has been lifted, the ink has been dried,' as the Muslims say. A world where everything exists simultaneously, eternally, and necessarily, where time has been exposed as an illusion and nothing exists except insofar as it is perceived by a conscious mind."

I glanced at my watch with growing despair: it was now after 4:30. In a few minutes, thousands of office workers would clog the streets of Boston and the bridges and highways around it. Time would be exposed as an illusion, all motion would cease, and it would be a marvelous coincidence if we ever made it back to Cambridge. In the rear-view mirror I glimpsed Borges in his tattered coat, his stick wobbling in front of him, drifting into the artifice of eternity. We plunged across the bridge, cars and trucks lurching and honking their way around us, as if daring me to let the Galaxie obliterate them. The car in front of us slammed on its brakes: I dodged into the next lane, desperately putting all my faith in the concave side mirror, even though I knew that the image displayed there, like so many of life's hazards, appeared smaller than actual size. In the distance ahead I could see the beginning of a huge traffic jam.

Borges, innocent of my struggles, seemed again to be dwelling on The Great Abdul and the mystery of his untimely death. "As usual," he said, "the solution will be in plain view."

The sudden shifts from one topic to another were starting to annoy me. "What does the story of the two dreamers have to do with The Great Abdul?" I asked Borges.

"Like the characters in the story," he said, "Lieutenant McGarry and I have related our dreams to each other. And the lieutenant's dream, like that of the Chief of Police in the story, has inspired me to look for the solution in my own back yard, and not to base my investigation on appearances, which I can't see—and which, as I should have known, are a distraction, if not an illusion."

I sensed an infinite regress. "If the appearances are an illusion," I asked him, "then what is the illusion?"

"It's an illusion, of course."

I had walked into that trap with my eyes open. Behind me, I could see Borges laughing to himself as if this little joke was the punch line he'd been building up to the whole time. "Magicians use mirrors for a reason," he said.

Just then we could have used some mirrors, or a magic carpet, or perhaps a little levitation. As I feared, our escape from the city had been too long delayed. Once across the bridge, the Galaxie had shuddered to a halt and come to rest in the eternal gridlock of rush-hour traffic, which never rushes but creeps across the landscape like Zeno's tortoise. Borges had entertained me with his excursion from Lieutenant McGarry to the *Arabian Nights* and idealist metaphysics and then back again to The Great Abdul. But now, in the absence of mirrors (other than my rear-view, in which I kept an eye on his fading smile), he seemed to be running down like the day itself. I tried to keep him talking, but it was a losing battle. Maybe he felt he'd said too much—sometimes a poet should keep his speculations to himself—or maybe he was just too tired to say any more. For an instant I thought I saw a grimace of despair cross his face. It had been a long afternoon, and as the sun dropped from the sky, our world was mutating in ways I could observe but he could only imagine. Shadows lengthened and reached across the road; the river sparkled with sunset and faded to gray; a pale moon floated along the edge of the earth. Borges sensed the approach of evening and discreetly fell silent.

He revived after a dinner of baked cod, parsleyed potatoes and asparagus tips, prepared by a neighbor lady who'd been hired to cook the Borges's meals four nights a week. At nine o'clock, after Señora Borges had retired to her room, Borges and I settled into our favorite chairs to have our way with another bottle of port. It was an aged Sandeman, rich and pungent, just the thing to warm our hearts after the journey to hell and back that afternoon. For a few minutes we were able to forget about the Chief of Police and Lieutenant McGarry and The Great Abdul and his gruesome fate.

Then Borges broke the spell. "Have you been enjoying Scheherazade's little detective story?" he asked.

"It's entertaining," I said. "Whether it's a reflection of reality, I don't know."

"Let's hope not!" he laughed. "Some say art should hold a mirror up to nature. Plato declared that nature itself is an imitation, unworthy of further reflection in art. On balance I think Plato had it right. The proper subject of art—even a detective story—isn't reality as we know it, but the world of uncreated ideas, the world of as if's and might have beens. So be careful that you don't wish those potentialities into being. Every detective story is an uncommitted crime."

I emptied the rest of the port into his glass. "That's the end of the port," I said. "Unless you have another bottle somewhere."

"No," he said. "And we won't be needing any more for the sake of The Great Abdul."

"Why do you say that?"

"Don't you remember? Immediately after the murder, the Chief of Police demanded that it be solved within three days. This is the third night. Therefore I predict that tonight the solution to the mystery will be revealed."

Scheherazade tapped on Borges's door shortly before ten o'clock, with a gleam of triumph in her eyes that flickered back at me like the sequins on her black evening gown. "The investigation has taken a dramatic turn," she announced, slipping into her usual chair. "As you know, I

informed Lieutenant McGarry about the demon woman
and the threats she made when she burst into our rehearsal.
He sent two detectives to search her house in Concord.
They found nothing, naturally—she is no fool. But they
watched her comings and goings from a hiding place across
the street, and before long she hurried out, climbed in her
car and sped away. And the detectives followed her—right
to Ivan Morloff's door in Charlestown!

"You'll recall that Ivan Morloff was my husband's
former master. Morloff's house sits by itself at the end of a
narrow *cul de sac* which branches off from a main street.
The demon woman parked her car on the main street and
walked toward Morloff's house, with the two detectives
following close behind. When she saw the detectives, she
ran to Ivan Morloff's door; Morloff let her in and quickly
locked the door behind him. The detectives radioed back to
Lieutenant McGarry, who ordered them to search the
house. And can you guess what they found in a closet in
Ivan Morloff's bedroom? The blood-stained costume that
had been worn by my husband's murderer, rolled up and
stuffed into a box."

"Did Morloff offer any explanation?" Borges asked.

"He claims he found the box wedged in his door the
morning after the murder. He says he never opened it."

"Did the police find any other evidence?"

"In the demon woman's purse, they found a letter to
her from Morloff, in which he urged her to come to his
house as soon as possible."

"Then the crime has been solved," Borges said. He
rose and acknowledged Scheherazade's triumph with a short
bow. "It was a conspiracy between Janice Brown and Ivan
Morloff, with the actual killing carried out by Janice Brown,

disguised as Bruno Eissler, as you conjectured last night. Congratulations on your superb detective work!"

Scheherazade fluttered her false eyelashes and beamed like a ballerina. Beneath her mask of face paint, rouge and eye shadow, I believe she actually blushed. Another round of mutual flattery and congratulation followed, at the end of which she leaned forward to plant a kiss on Borges's cheek and then, without another word, disappeared out the door.

"So that's how the story ends," I said.

"Not exactly," Borges smiled, wiping his cheek with a handkerchief. "You'll recall that the Chief of Police allowed three days to solve the crime. Thus the story won't end until tomorrow morning when the inquest is held at the Medical Examiner's office."

"But you said yourself that the crime has been solved. You're not planning to go to the inquest, are you?"

"Oh, yes," he said. "I wouldn't miss it for the world. You're free tomorrow morning, I assume?"

∞

They say there's no greater illusion than love. All the magicians in the world couldn't duplicate its legerdemain. Houdini himself, who made an elephant disappear before thousands of spectators, would have traded all his secrets for a lover's glance. But if love is an illusion, in an old man it's an illusion verging on madness.

Or so you'd assume. In this, as in all other things, it was Borges's destiny to be different. After returning to Argentina, he married a lovely young woman with whom he would spend the happiest years of his life. By all accounts he was a man transformed, who enjoyed every minute of the time that was left to him. And why not? If time is an infinite number of discrete moments, why not slice them into as many pieces as possible? Only love can stop time's arrow.

Nilsa has started coming more often, almost every day, an angel of mercy bringing relief from unbearable pain. As she works on my back, she tells me about her family in Nicaragua, where the mountainsides are so steep, the roads so rocky, that her village can be reached only on foot. Her journey to the United States through Mexico was a near-death experience that included riding on the top of a freight train fending off marauders with a machete. She is strong and beautiful and I want to spend the rest of my life with her. Before I put that plan into action, I need to talk to my daughters: not to ask their permission, but to let them know that nothing will stand in my way. I know they will see it as a betrayal of their mother. They believe—especially Ingrid—that after the accident I deserve to be unhappy for the rest of my life. Most of the time I believe that too, even though the police said it wasn't my fault. Nilsa is my only hope for release from the cycle of regret.

I'll never forget the day Borges and I attended the official inquest into the death of The Great Abdul. It was only a few weeks since Borges had told the faux Unitarian Reverend Pendragon (a little too cavalierly, I thought) that the meaning of death, if it has one, is meaninglessness, and scarcely two weeks since he'd suffered through his dark night of the soul, when his mind's eyes opened to the quixotic vanity of a lifetime spent dreaming of ideas he thought were merely philosophical or literary when in fact they were real and could kill people. He believed that the murders of Achille Toulou, Stephen Albert and Mary Talbot were committed for the sole purpose of planting a pattern—that is, a meaning—in his mind. By grasping that pattern, he'd become an accomplice in the murders of three innocent people; and this was a sin, he said, for which there could be no absolution. Was that the price he had to pay for trying to cheat death of its meaning? Now, shaken by his experiences, he seemed willing to give death its due.

I picked him up at 8:00 a.m. to drive to Boston for the inquest. His mood was subdued and grimly determined, as if he'd made up his mind to perform a distasteful but necessary task. He spoke of death and was careful not to belittle it. The gruesome image of The Great Abdul's execution hovered in his mind's eye. He was about to enter the most treacherous labyrinth of all, the labyrinth of the law, where a meaning must be assigned to every death. To my surprise, the path he chose led back to Thomas De Quincey.

"De Quincey was a great stylist," he said as the Galaxie rumbled toward Boston, "though hardly a moral philosopher. He was a drug addict who viewed life as a manifestation of literature. Remember his essay on 'Murder Considered As One of the Fine Arts'? I now regret basing my first investigation on such a shallow piece of writing; nevertheless I believe it may be the key to the present case. In a convoluted, backwards way—which is what you'd expect after listening to the dizzying tales of Scheherazade—De Quincey's aesthetic approach to crime, though based on a false premise, may lead to the solution."

"I don't think I followed that," I admitted.

"Murder, no matter how cleverly contrived, is never a work of art," he said. "The killer who conceives it as such is sure to be found out."

Illusionists (Concluded)

On the morning of the inquest, Borges and I arrived at the Suffolk County Health Services Building shortly before 9:00 o'clock. We found our way into a drafty, high-windowed room that was furnished with a large desk for the Medical Examiner, an array of tables and chairs for interested parties, a lectern, and benches for the press, the homeless, and the morbidly curious. At the table closest to the Medical Examiner's desk sat Lieutenant McGarry, his face buried in papers as he reviewed the results of his investigation. Scheherazade sat alone at the next table, quietly sobbing in a black dress, black stockings, a black pill-box hat and a black veil, in case anyone wondered whether she might be the widow. She lifted her veil and nodded in our direction as we sat down in the first row of chairs. I had no idea what to expect, never having attended an inquest before. All I knew was that it was an administrative proceeding aimed at establishing the cause of death of Leon Gogol (a/k/a The Great Abdul). The suspects and other interested parties were invited but would not be required to participate.

A phalanx of uniformed guards ushered in the current suspects, accompanied by their attorneys, and deposited them at separate tables. Janice Brown—Scheherazade's 'demon woman'—was a thin, tense blonde with a mad gleam in her eyes. She might have been attractive if she hadn't seemed so frightened and distraught. Her lawyer huddled close beside her, a gray-haired, gray-eyed man of about sixty in a gray pin-striped suit—I'll call him Mr. Gray—who whispered in her ear and ignored everyone else. Ivan Morloff, bent over from arthritis, looked closer to eighty than to sixty-five. Even so, the guards kept a tight grip on him when they escorted him in, as if they thought he might make a run for it. His lawyer was a dwarfish man named Arthur Kleinzach—he couldn't have been over five feet tall—with an impish grin and a chronically sarcastic tone of voice. Unlike Janice Brown's lawyer, he never stopped talking and he was always in motion, his little legs propelling him around the room like a wind-up doll.

The magician's assistant Bruno Eissler—he'd been released from jail that morning after Brown and Morloff were formally charged—came in smiling and joking with a ruddy-faced Irishman named Joseph J. O'Doyle whose lapels were as wide as his grin and who looked more like a professional gambler than an attorney, though he might have been both. It was Eissler's first public appearance since the night of the murder, when he'd been dragged off the stage in the robes of Masrur the Executioner, streaked with makeup, groggy with chloroform and apparently scared out of his wits. He looked relaxed and self-confident now, in his stylish suit (stylish in those days meant something you might see on Ringo Starr or Ronald McDonald), his bangly jewelry and his shiny boots. You could hardly blame him for being overjoyed at his reversal of fortune, but the flashy dress and demeanor struck me as unseemly at an inquest, especially with the widow sitting a few feet away. I noticed Scheherazade grimacing under her veil as Eissler and his attorney found seats in the first row of chairs.

A bailiff called the room to order and a short, dark-haired woman of about fifty stepped in and perched behind the front desk. She nodded at the spectators and the bailiff announced: "No. 68-40639, Inquest into the death of Leon Gogol a/k/a The Great Abdul. Anne Marie Russo, M.D., Suffolk County Medical Examiner, presiding."

After a few preliminaries, which Dr. Russo, in her soft, even voice, dispatched with chilling efficiency, Lieutenant McGarry walked to the lectern and began to introduce himself.

"Excuse me, lieutenant," Dr. Russo interrupted. "Who are all these people?" She gestured toward the tables in front of her desk. "Why are they here?"

"The widow, Mrs. Gogol, is here"—the lieutenant pointed to Scheherazade—"and the two individuals, Janice Brown and Ivan Morloff, who have been charged with murder in the first degree, and their attorneys."

Mr. Gray nodded respectfully to the Medical Examiner. Morloff's attorney, the dwarfish Arthur Kleinzach, jumped to his feet and rattled off a string of objections.

Dr. Russo cut him off. "Sit down, please."

"Also present is Bruno Eissler," the lieutenant went on, "who had previously been charged with the crime. All charges against Mr. Eissler have been dropped."

Bruno Eissler's ruddy-faced attorney grinned at the Medical Examiner and lurched upwards. "Joseph J. O'Doyle, your honor—"

"Sit down."

She glared at Borges, who faced her with his most benevolent smile. "And who are you, if I may ask?"

"My name is Jorge Luis Borges," he said, somehow perceiving that the question was directed to him. "I am a poet of modest talent and accomplishment. I was an eyewitness to the murder. Since then I have been consulted by the widow and have attempted to provide guidance to the police, who, unfortunately, have not seen fit to follow my advice. I know who murdered the unfortunate Mr. Gogol."

Dr. Russo frowned at Lieutenant McGarry as if he were to blame for inviting this cast of characters into her hearing room. "The sole purpose of this proceeding," she said, "is to establish the cause of the decedent's death, and to supplement the pathologist's conclusions with extrinsic evidence, if any, relevant to that determination. Parties other than the police are permitted to attend on condition that they do not disrupt the proceedings. Is that clear?"

Everyone nodded their agreement. "Now," she said, "there's no dispute about the cause of death, is there? The pathologist concluded that death resulted from sudden decapitation."

"That is correct," the lieutenant said. "The decedent's head was chopped off in front of hundreds of people."

"Is there any evidence that death occurred prior to, or after, the decapitation, or as the result of any other cause?"

"No, ma'am."

"Don't call me *ma'am*."

"Yes, your honor."

"Don't call me that, either. I'm not a judge."

"Yes, Dr. Russo."

"Continue, then."

Lieutenant McGarry proceeded with a detailed description of The Great Abdul's decapitation, the chaotic scene that ensued, the arrest of Bruno Eissler, and the subsequent investigation leading to charges being brought against Janice Brown and Ivan Morloff. Whenever he mentioned Ivan Morloff, Kleinzach would grunt sarcastically and leer at the spectators as if the suggestion that his client had anything to do with the murder was an outrage. By the time the lieutenant accused Morloff of conspiring to murder The Great Abdul, Kleinzach had worked himself into such a state—pounding the table, stamping his tiny feet, throwing up his hands—that he could hardly stay in his seat.

"That's enough!" Dr. Russo snapped. "Save your theatrics for the trial."

"Your honor—excuse me: Dr. Russo—I apologize." Kleinzach was on his feet now, pacing in circles in front of the lectern. "The point I'm trying to make is that there shouldn't be a trial, at least not of my client. Look at him! He's a feeble old man who could hardly make it into the hearing room without help from the guards." Kleinzach glared at the lieutenant. "You say he's a magician. Do you think he can kill people by hocus-pocus?"

"Appearances can be deceiving."

"Yes, and as usual it's the police who are doing the deceiving."

The lieutenant's face reddened. "Do I have to put up with this?"

"Mr. Kleinzach," Dr. Russo said, "we're not here to listen to you insult the police. Sit down."

"I don't know about you, doctor, but I don't believe in magic. And you know what? The case against my client is all smoke and mirrors."

The lieutenant waved a plastic bag that had something wadded up inside it. "This bloody robe was found in Mr. Morloff's house—"

"A bloody robe! Don't you know any new tricks, lieutenant? God knows you've pulled enough rabbits out of your hat over the years—"

The Medical Examiner slapped her hand down on the desk. "Sit down or I'll have you removed!"

Kleinzach sat down and gave Morloff a comforting pat on the back.

"This bloody robe was found in Mr. Morloff's house," the lieutenant repeated calmly, "and a letter from him to Miss Brown—"

"I never sent that letter!" Morloff croaked.

"Be quiet, Ivan!" Kleinzach clamped his hand across his client's mouth. "Let the record reflect that my client spoke out emotionally and against the advice of counsel."

"Duly noted," Dr. Russo said.

Lieutenant McGarry continued: "The letter, which was signed 'Morloff,' asked Miss Brown to come to his house as soon as possible. It was postmarked Saturday morning and found in her handbag on Monday afternoon."

"Just for the record," Kleinzach said, "my client never wrote or mailed that letter."

"Mr. Morloff hated Leon Gogol and publicly threatened to kill him. He believed that Mr. Gogol had driven him from the stage, appropriating his illusions, his stage name and his very persona as a magician."

"Pure fiction!" Kleinzach grunted, shaking his head.

"He secluded himself in his house, nursing his bitterness and lust for revenge, until one day, just two weeks ago, a stranger knocked on his door and enlisted him in a diabolical plot."

"A fairy tale!" Kleinzach muttered, loud enough to be heard in the back. "Right out of a book!"

"The stranger who knocked on the door was none other than Janice Brown. Leon Gogol, posing as an Arabian sheik, had pretended to marry her, though he already had one wife, if not more. When she learned the truth she was beside herself with fury. She located Morloff and the two of them plotted their revenge. One afternoon she stormed into the theater where Gogol was rehearsing with his wife and Mr. Eissler. 'Ivan Morloff despises you for what you did,' she told him, 'and wishes you an early and excruciating death. He attends every one of your performances in anticipation of the inevitable day when you will make a fatal mistake and reveal yourself as a fraud and a charlatan. I know now that our marriage is one of your tricks. My whole life is an illusion, as yours will be soon. You have made a fatal mistake, and you will not live long to regret it.'"

Kleinzach was on his feet, running his fingertips across Morloff's balding scalp as he scowled at Lieutenant McGarry. "Does my client have horns?" he demanded, winking at the spectators. "Look at him! Do you see horns?"

The crowd erupted in laughter as the lieutenant shouted angrily and the Medical Examiner, banging on her desk, ordered the bailiff to eject Kleinzach from the building. He resisted, ducking under the table like a little boy, and when the guards finally clamped their arms around him he called out his demand that the hearing be adjourned, since his client had a right to counsel. Dr. Russo called all the attorneys forward, including Kleinzach, who could hardly see over her desk, and after a heated discussion Kleinzach was allowed to remain at the table beside Ivan Morloff, flanked by a pair of guards.

To my surprise, Borges chose this moment to enter the fray. Leaning forward on his walking stick, he lurched to his feet and waited until the noise died down. "Dr. Russo," he said in his quiet voice, "if I may, I think I can put an end to this quarreling. I know who the murderer is."

"You're the poet?" Dr. Russo said, wrinkling her brow.

"Yes," he said. "And a detective of sorts."

"And—excuse me, but are you blind?"

"Yes, I am."

"Dr. Russo"—Eissler's attorney, Joseph J. O'Doyle, rose to object—"I can't see how anything this man says could be material to the matter at hand. A blind man—"

"I agree, I wholeheartedly agree," sputtered Kleinzach, wagging his head. "Irrelevant and immaterial."

"I know who the murderer is," Borges smiled. "What could be more relevant than that?"

There was no graceful way to dismiss him. Dr. Russo shook her head in exasperation. "All right, Mr. Borges," she said. "Tell us what you know." She signaled to Lieutenant McGarry to sit down.

One hand on his walking stick, the other clutching my elbow, Borges stumbled to the lectern and turned his clouded eyes toward the Medical Examiner. "In March of 1918," he began, "at the Wood Green Theater in London, a magician who went by the name Chung Ling Soo—he was known as the 'marvelous Chinese conjuror'—was shot dead on stage while performing his most famous illusion, 'Condemned to Death by the Boxers.' This artist had enjoyed an enormous success by imitating a popular Chinese magician named Ching Ling Foo, mimicking his name and his act and finally usurping his place in the public imagination. On the night of his death, six assistants, simulating a firing squad, shot at him with muzzle-loading rifles. All but one of the rifles was loaded with blanks, the other with a live bullet which had been inspected by a knowledgeable member of the audience. The magician was supposed to catch the bullet in mid-air, but on this occasion it entered his chest and he died soon afterwards."

Dr. Russo nodded soberly, and the attorneys, following her lead, seemed to be intent on giving Borges a respectful hearing. "The tragedy was front page news all over Europe," he went on, "even as its armies slaughtered each other in the last spasms of the Great War. I recall reading about the incident as a boy waiting out the war with my family in Geneva. The question on everyone's lips was, How could such a thing happen? Did the famous Chinese conjuror commit suicide? Or was he murdered by the assistant who fired the fatal shot, or by his wife, who had loaded the guns? Or by someone else shooting from a hidden location in the theater—possibly his former master, Ching Ling Foo, who was a skilled conjuror and had every reason to seek revenge? An accident seemed out of the question: Chung Ling Soo had performed the trick hundreds of times."

Borges raised his walking stick and held it out like a rifle. "At a coroner's inquest much like this one, a forensics expert examined the rifle and explained what had gone wrong. The trick was meant to work like this:"—he turned around and aimed the stick at O'Doyle, pointing along it with his left hand—"The bullet was loaded into a dummy barrel and a blank charge was fired from the ramrod tube, giving the appearance that the bullet had been fired when in fact it never left the gun. But due to Chung Ling Soo's own carelessness there had been a build-up of gunpowder in the back of the dummy barrel. On this occasion it ignited and caused the real bullet to fire. The coroner ruled 'death by misadventure,' and that was supposed to be the end of the story."

"Put that thing down!" O'Doyle demanded, flashing a scowl around the room.

Borges lowered the stick and went on: "Not everyone was satisfied with this verdict. In the course of the investigation it had been discovered that Chung Ling Soo's whole life was a deception. His real name was William Robinson; he was an American from New York, not a conjuror from China. Robinson was married to one of his assistants, but he had another wife in London and another who'd been left behind in America. In his professional life, William Robinson had been an impostor like Leon Gogol, with a fake name, a fake nationality, and an act he'd stolen from a man more talented than himself. He could get away with this imposture because of the real Chinese magician's shyness and reticence. After a while the public started thinking he *was* Ching Ling Foo; they bought the copy and discarded the original."

"Dr. Russo"—O'Doyle was on his feet—"This has gone on long enough. We're wasting precious time." He glanced down at his client, Bruno Eissler, whose eyes, I noticed, had lost their merry twinkle.

"I'm just getting to the good part," Borges said.

Dr. Russo frowned. "One more minute. Sit down, Mr. O'Doyle."

"Thank you," Borges nodded. "One day, I believe, Chung Ling Soo began to suspect that his own assistant would do to him what he had done to Ching Ling Foo. He became convinced that the assistant was studying his act with the aim of stealing it and driving him from the stage. He confided in his wife, never once suspecting that she would conspire with the assistant to kill him. To the assistant it must have seemed the opportunity of a lifetime, the opportunity not only to usurp his master but to destroy him in full view of the public. It would be an artistic triumph, the ultimate illusion that would catapult him to the pinnacle of his profession. And the best way to do it—the only way, as the wife explained—was to carry out his role as the man who pulled the trigger, or brought down the sword, as the case may be."

Borges had advanced toward his provocative conclusion against a crescendo of hostile noises from Bruno Eissler and Joseph J. O'Doyle. At the mention of swordplay, the genial attorney sprang to his feet like an enraged beast. "Wait a minute!" he snarled, taking a step toward Borges. "Who the hell are you, anyway?"

Borges smiled as if the question was beneath him.

O'Doyle aimed his red face at the Medical Examiner. "I object to the participation of this man," he said, "who seems to have wandered in off the street. He's talking nonsense—"

"I want to hear what he has to say," Dr. Russo cut him off.

"Whoever he is, he has no standing to speak at this hearing." O'Doyle glowered at Borges and took another step toward him. "What are you doing here?"

"Back off, Mr. O'Doyle," Dr. Russo ordered. "And sit down."

O'Doyle complied, turning his scowl on Kleinzach, who'd gone back into motion, giggling and clapping his hands as he jiggled his tiny feet and nudged Ivan Morloff with his elbow. Mr. Gray allowed himself a faint smile as he patted Janice Brown on the wrist. Scheherazade sat motionless behind her black veil. Bruno Eissler looked like he might be sick.

"Mr. Borges," the Medical Examiner said, choosing her words carefully, "are you suggesting that Mr. Gogol's fate somehow reflected the death of this so-called Chinese conjuror fifty years ago?"

"More than mere reflection," Borges said. "Conscious mimicry would be a better description."

She grimaced in disbelief. "Mimicry by the killer?"

"Precisely."

"Why would the killer give himself away like that? Assuming there was a killer."

Her tone of voice had become incredulous. O'Doyle shot a triumphant glance at Kleinzach.

Borges raised his walking stick and waved it like a magic wand. "A magician is a magician," he said, "only as long as he has an audience that knows he's doing magic. If you create an illusion and everyone is deceived by it—if they think what they've seen is not an illusion but a depiction of reality—then you're not a magician; you may be a prophet, perhaps, or a great statesman, but not an artist. A work of art must have a beholder who knows that what he's experiencing is a work of art."

"I think we're going pretty far afield here, Mr. Borges—"

It was Borges's turn to interrupt. "And so to answer your question," he said, turning around to face O'Doyle. "You asked what I'm doing here and I will tell you."

"Mr. Borges, that's enough!"

"I sat in the audience the night The Great Abdul died, along with everyone else, but I wasn't fooled by appearances. I knew that what was unfolding on the stage was an illusion. Anyone familiar with the story of Chung Ling Soo would have recognized that. And so I—or someone like me, who knew the story of Chung Ling Soo— had to be there. I was the beholder whose presence was required to make the illusion a success."

O'Doyle laughed derisively. "That's the most ridiculous thing I've ever heard!"

"It was for this reason that the illusionist made sure I received a ticket."

Dr. Russo raised her eyebrows. "Is this true, Mr. O'Doyle? Did your client arrange for Mr. Borges to attend the performance?"

"Well, what if he did? How would he know that Mr. Borges, whoever he is, knew anything about this Chung Ling Soo? And even if he knew that, so what?" O'Doyle leaned toward the spectators as if he were arguing to a jury. "One thing's certain," he went on. "Whatever happened on that stage, Mr. Borges didn't see it. The man's blind; he's admitted as much. Yet we're supposed to believe"—his voice dripped with sarcasm—"that Mr. Eissler arranged for him to attend the performance because he, Mr. Borges, the blind man, out of everyone in the audience—everyone in Boston, apparently—would know that the whole thing was a trick, an elaborate way to murder Mr. Gogol in some kind of diabolical re-enactment of a crime that may or may not have been committed fifty years ago. And not only that: we're supposed to believe that Mr. Eissler, though he invited the eyewitness, so to speak, still expected to get away with his crime, because that eyewitness, Mr. Borges, though he knew it was a trick, would allow himself to be fooled by it. Mr. Borges, maybe you can tell us—why would a murderer have taken that chance?"

"My reputation is well known," Borges replied softly. "An artist capable of conceiving this illusion would have known that I'd notice the resemblance to Chung Ling Soo and at a subconscious level perceive the murder as a trick. But I was expected to suspend my disbelief, and not to admit, even to myself, that I had done so. That's what every artist expects of his audience."

O'Doyle rolled his eyes in an exquisite blend of pity and contempt. His Clarence Darrow act had worked its magic. Bruno Eissler leaned back in his chair and allowed himself a smile, and Scheherazade lifted her veil to snicker at Borges. Kleinzach sat quietly with downcast eyes, ignoring Morloff's anxious whispers, while Mr. Gray struggled to calm Janice Brown. And the Medical Examiner herself, as she weighed her options, wore an expression that could only be described as dark and determined. The next time she opened her mouth, it seemed certain, she would order Borges ejected from the hearing, if not thrown in jail. But just when all appeared lost, the aforesaid Joseph J. O'Doyle, Esquire, who had so clearly won the day with his oratory, came to the rescue by making the single biggest mistake a lawyer can make—the mistake that every novice attorney is warned against and yet is fated to commit, sooner or later, in a fit of hubris. He asked one question too many.

"Mr. Borges," O'Doyle inquired in his most biting tone, "is there the slightest shred of evidence that this elaborate fantasy of yours is true?"

"The evidence," Borges said with a smile, "is in plain view."

The Medical Examiner, weary though she was of Borges's conundrums, couldn't let this comment pass. She eyed him severely. "Exactly what are you talking about, Mr. Borges?"

"Perhaps I should say that the lack of evidence—which is often the best kind of evidence—is in plain view."

"There is no evidence, then?"

"The lack of evidence *is* the evidence. We are dealing with an illusion of an illusion by a master illusionist. The only evidence one would expect to find is evidence that incriminates others, which is exactly what we have."

Kleinzach skittered out of his seat and around the lectern. "Your honor—Dr. Russo—if I may say so, I agree. There's no evidence that Ivan Morloff or Janice Brown ever set foot in that theater."

"Unless," Borges added, "we accept the preposterous notion that Miss Brown drugged Mr. Eissler, dressed up in his costume and flawlessly performed his role in the show."

"No more preposterous," growled O'Doyle, whose color had risen to a fiery red, "than Mr. Borges's fantasies about what my client is supposed to have done."

"Does anyone seriously believe," Borges asked, ignoring O'Doyle, "that someone who is not an actor or a magician could master that complicated role simply by observing a few performances from the audience? Mr. Kleinzach is right: that sort of thing happens only in fairy tales—in this case a tale told by Mr. Eissler's mistress, Scheherazade."

Dr. Russo gasped and peered over the top of her glasses. Her suspension of disbelief had reached its limit. "Scheherazade?"

"That's my stage name," Scheherazade admitted, springing to her feet. She pulled back her veil and bowed.

"You're the widow, I assume? Mrs. Gogol? And you go by 'Scheherazade?'"

"Yes, it's my stage name."

"And are you Mr. Eissler's mistress?"

"Objection!" O'Doyle exploded. "I object to that characterization—"

"Keep quiet, Mr. O'Doyle. Mrs. Gogol?"

Scheherazade looked away. "I thought I was more than just his mistress."

Excitement sizzled through the crowd. "Now wait a minute," O'Doyle bellowed. "This doesn't prove anything." He glared at Scheherazade. "Didn't you tell the police that two weeks ago Janice Brown came to the theater during a rehearsal and shouted threats at The Great Abdul in the name of Ivan Morloff?"

"Yes, yes," Scheherazade murmured. "I was there."

"You were there," Borges said. "And so was Bruno Eissler—and oh, yes, Mr. Gogol, who is now dead, and no one else. How convenient."

Janice Brown, her face twisted with hatred, lunged toward Scheherazade. "It never happened!" she shouted as Mr. Gray pulled her back. "She's lying!"

"Of course she's lying." Borges smiled at Janice Brown as if she'd called attention to a charming plot device. "It's one of her tales."

Scheherazade glared at Borges as if she were going to tear out his heart, then lowered her eyes. The Medical

Examiner's mind must have been reeling. The inquest, ordinarily a routine administrative hearing, had been diverted into a labyrinth from which, it must have seemed, she would never be able to extricate herself. She took a deep breath and plunged ahead. "Mr. Borges, are you saying this was all a trick?"

"Not a trick, Dr. Russo. An illusion. Performed in the Alhambra Theater at a time when the Chief of Police was certain to be there—a bold but predictable touch!—and then elaborated for his feckless subordinates. And now, after an attempt to extend it here, it appears to be unraveling."

"We're after facts here," she said, her voice faltering. "Not illusions."

Borges gestured with his walking stick like a professor in front of a blackboard. "There are two types of illusions," he said. "In the first type, the magician shows you something impossible—a lady being sawed in half, a flock of pigeons flying out of a hat—and tricks you into believing what you see. In the second and more difficult type, the magician makes you *disbelieve* what you see with your own eyes. He does this by making the ordinary and obvious seem impossible."

He pointed the stick at Bruno Eissler. "That's what Mr. Eissler did in this case. He killed Mr. Gogol in front of hundreds of spectators and then set up circumstances that made it impossible for those spectators to believe what they had seen. The illusion had several steps. First, as in any magic show, the audience thought they were watching an illusion: they were ready to believe the impossible and doubt the obvious. By actually decapitating his victim"—Borges swept the stick down in imitation of the fatal blow—"Mr.

Eissler made the impossible real; and then, by skillfully manipulating the evidence, he made the real impossible."

"Mr. Borges, please!" Dr. Russo said. "You're going to hit someone with that thing."

"I beg your pardon, doctor." He set the tip of the stick back on the floor where it belonged. "This last and most difficult step was accomplished by focusing attention on the blood-soaked robe. The robe had to be blood-soaked—that was essential to the plot. But the robe Mr. Eissler was wearing when they found him unconscious in the closet had to be spotless—that was key to his eventual exoneration. The police, having watched him decapitate The Great Abdul, could hardly be blamed for ignoring this discrepancy: they thought it was part of the trick. That too was essential to the plot, since his arrest gave Mr. Eissler a perfect alibi for the next critical step in the illusion: the removal of the real blood-soaked robe from the theater."

Lieutenant McGarry spoke up for the first time since Borges took the podium. "The police didn't ignore any evidence," he said. "We're proud of the work we did on this case."

Borges silenced him with a dismissive wave of the hand. "Someone smuggled that costume out of the theater and left it on Mr. Morloff's doorstep. Janice Brown, if she were the murderer, would not have done that; nor would Mr. Morloff, obviously. Mr. Eissler, as we have seen, was in jail. The only person who could have done it"—he paused, swiveled, and pointed his stick at the woman in black— "was Scheherazade."

All eyes were on the grieving widow. "You, you!" she stammered, sneering at Borges. "You're a liar! A charlatan! Everything about you is a lie!"

"Keep quiet!" Dr. Russo demanded.

"She is a woman of extraordinary imagination and cunning," Borges went on. "She hated her husband, and like the wife of Chung Ling Soo she craved the attentions of a younger man—at first, perhaps, only as an audience for her fantastic tales. There's something irresistible, almost erotic, in her compulsive storytelling—undoubtedly Mr. Eissler, in his vanity, succumbed quickly to the nightly entertainments. As time went on her stories became more murderous and convoluted, tales within tales, like facing mirrors. The superimposition of illusions—actually killing the victim while only seeming to kill him in a performance everyone assumed to be an illusion—was her masterstroke. Bruno Eissler became her unwitting tool and performed his role flawlessly, as she directed. When he was arrested, she couldn't bear losing her audience. In desperation she made nightly trips to my apartment in an effort to lure me into her labyrinth of lies as she had lured Mr. Eissler—"

"No!" Scheherazade protested. "I only told Bruno those stories because he threatened to kill me if I stopped. They were just stories, fantasies, that's all. I didn't know he would actually carry them out."

"Nonsense, madam! You told him those stories to indoctrinate him in the plot you had devised to kill your husband."

"No!" she screamed. "It was all his idea! The whole thing was his idea!"

Bruno Eissler sat shaking his head in disbelief and disillusionment. Borges, who couldn't see him, nevertheless pointed directly at him with his stick; and then he laughed, rather inappropriately, I thought, in light of the accusations he was making. "Mr. Eissler," he said. "You had never heard of Chung Ling Soo before today, had you? And you had no inkling, I'm sure, that your mistress, the woman we know as Scheherazade, based the script for her husband's demise on that obscure chapter of magical history. Or that she then invited me to the execution, knowing that I would notice the resemblances to Chung Ling Soo. And you are probably asking yourself, as Dr. Russo did: Why would a killer do that?"

Borges started swinging his stick around, rather dangerously, everyone thought, judging from their expressions. He swung it toward Eissler, and then toward Scheherazade; and the two guards who sat flanking Kleinzach exchanged glances indicating that if he came any closer they would jump up and grab the stick out of his hand. I stepped up beside him so I could protect him in the event of a scuffle. "Why would a killer do that?"—he repeated—"if not for the purpose of flaunting a masterpiece? It was the kind of bold mistake an artist must make if he or she aspires to greatness. Unfortunately for both of you I was also the one person who could see the crime for what it was. Scheherazade, like her namesake, had been relegated to the ignominious role of sex slave; she hated her husband with a smoldering passion. She had written the script for his magic show—indeed for his entire career—and got no credit for it. The script for his murder, she resolved, would prove her worth as an artist. It would prove that she was a great illusionist in her own right, greater than Chung Ling Soo, greater than The Great Abdul—and yes, greater than you, Mr. Eissler."

The stick swung to a halt in front of Eissler's incredulous eyes. "For although your mimicry of the death of Chung Ling Soo may have been a mistake," Borges continued, "it was not an innocent one on your mistress's part. It was her insurance policy—part of the illusion, as she conceived it. If the plot to implicate Ivan Morloff and Janice Brown failed, the connection to Chung Ling Soo would provide a context and a set of motives that would point directly at you. You are the illusionist, she a lowly female assistant—an enlisted storyteller at best. She would be able to say just what she's saying now: the whole thing was your idea."

Bruno Eissler flew out of his seat before anyone could stop him. He leaped on Scheherazade and knocked her to the floor, brandishing a small curved knife. "You've told your last tale, Scheherazade!" he cried as he raised the knife.

Miraculously, Borges's walking stick, darting out like a cobra, found its mark in the middle of Eissler's forehead, stunning him just long enough for the guards to crush him in a flying tackle before he could do any harm. The little knife, which was sharp enough to slit Scheherazade's throat, tumbled to the floor.

Borges stood unperturbed not three feet away, his hand resting lightly on the handle of his stick. To my credit, I cringed loyally beside him, though my instinct, guided by the advice of counsel, would have been to follow the example of Messrs. Kleinzach, O'Doyle and Gray, who leaped from their seats at the first sign of violence and bolted for the door.

By nine o'clock the next morning Borges's apartment was under siege by the press, demanding to know how he'd cracked the Gogol case. "I did it with mirrors," he'd told a *Globe* reporter the night before, and his boast made the first page of the morning edition. A desperate phone call jolted me from a dreamless sleep and summoned me to Cambridge. "I need to slip away from my palace for a while," he explained. Within the hour I tapped on his door and led him down the back stairs to the waiting Galaxie.

At the coffee shop I watched for Diotima but she was nowhere in sight. Instead we were waited on by a troll-like woman with untidy braids and teeth that looked like they fell out of a Cracker Jack box. She served our beverages— black coffee for me, maté for Borges—with an air of disdain that I attributed to Borges's habit of rolling his clouded eyes toward her as she served the other patrons. She must have thought he was ogling her.

"The last time we were here," Borges mused, "we were talking about illusion and her plain step-sister, reality, and the question of how to tell them apart." He took a long sip of his maté. "Not always an easy proposition, is it?"

Did he think I'd had nothing more important to think about in the past week than some remark of Maupassant's? "*On ne sait jamais,*" I said with a Gallic shrug.

"For example," he went on, "we'll probably never know whether Scheherazade put Bruno Eissler up to murdering her husband or whether she just went along with him, as she claimed."

It shocked me to hear him say that. "But yesterday," I protested, "you were sure it was all her idea!"

He smiled his most mischievous smile. "Was I? Or could I too have been dissembling? She said I was a liar, didn't she?" He bent toward me with his forefinger in the air. "I knew she would betray Eissler if I pushed her far enough. And then he would spring at her, and that would be as close as we'd ever get to a confession from either of

them. In the event"—he waved the forefinger menacingly—
"I was ready for Eissler with my walking stick."

I shook my head in disbelief. "So it was a trick!"

"Not a trick," he smiled. "An illusion. I was pitted
against a pair of masters who had attempted the boldest
illusion of all—the concealment of reality behind reality
itself."

We emptied our cups and stood up to leave. The
coffee shop had lost its charm, and not only because my
favorite waitress wasn't there: the danishes were stale, the
coffee weak—even the hot water for Borges's maté seemed
to be weak, judging by the way he sniffed at it—and the
service had been abominable. We paid our check, leaving a
smallish tip for the troll, and escaped just as she turned to
give us the evil eye. Outside, the sun was shining and
Borges wanted to walk around the block before climbing
back in the car. I led him down a street of gray, flat-roofed
houses, two or three stories high, noticing details he
couldn't see: a teenage couple holding hands on the other
side of the street; a squirrel spiraling up a tree; a bird
flittering outside a window while a cat crouched inside with
madness in her eyes. But there was another world on that
street that I wasn't aware of until Borges pointed it out, an
unseen world of equally sharp details—salt air blowing in
from the bay, school children shouting on a playground,
fish frying in a luncheonette—that were as striking to him
as the cat and the squirrel had been to me. He talked
constantly, but I'd had trouble paying attention since before
we left the coffee shop. My thoughts were full of Diotima's
absence. It was the first time she hadn't been there and I
was worried. I feared that the love of my life had been
replaced by a troll—or even worse, turned into one.

"The world is crowded with illusionists," Borges said as
we rounded a corner to a small commercial strip containing
a bar, a real estate office and a barber shop. "Husbands,
wives, fathers, politicians, statesmen, priests, teachers, artists
of all kinds. Lawyers who bend the truth, novelists who
imagine their own reality and call themselves realists,
theologians who argue for the existence of a God who, if
anyone accepted their arguments, could not possibly exist—
they are all illusionists. What do they have in common?
They are trying to pass off an imperfect copy of something
as the real thing."

In the window of the barber shop I caught a glimpse of
what I thought was Borges's face. In that reflection—
though not on his face when I checked it an instant later—I
saw an image of despair such as I'd never seen in him
before. The barber smiled and waved back with his
scissors, perhaps mistaking Borges for someone he knew.

Borges plodded ahead, tapping the sidewalk with his
cane. "Illusionists—and we are all illusionists—live in a
world of mimicry and deception, like the characters in the
Arabian Nights. They—we—are charlatans, courtesans,
tricksters, counterfeiters: mimics, in a word, of whatever is
truer or more real than our representation of it."

I guided him around the last corner into another block
of drab, flat-roofed houses. At the end of the street I could
see the Galaxie glistening in the sunlight. "We're not to
blame," he went on. "We use the tools that have been
given us—thought and memory, the illusionists that each of
us carries around inside of himself. They can make us
doubt what we see with our own eyes, and they can make us
believe in things that never were. Memory, at best, is a
mirror of past certainties, at worst a deceiver, a flatterer, a

betrayer; like any mirror, it deceives by offering us the appearance—the reflection, the copy—as the real thing. Thought is often called reflection: as such it's another form of duplication, like fathering children, and therefore an abomination. The notion that people might at this moment be reading my words—the thoughts I have recorded in my books—is as unbearable to me as a wilderness of mirrors."

Arriving at the car, we climbed inside and Borges kept talking. The pace of the past few days had caught up with me: I felt exhausted and all I wanted was to go home. I asked Borges if he wanted to go home, and he said no, he wanted to sit on the bench by the Charles River. I was too tired to object. I assumed he didn't want to go home to the news reporters, but as it turned out I was mistaken. He didn't want to go home to his wife.

"Yeats has a poem called 'The Gift of Harun Al-Rashid,'" he said as I drove around Porter Square. "He imagines himself a minor official in the court of the Caliph Harun al-Rashid, an aging scholar without a wife. The Caliph gives him a young girl to take as his bride, and every night she falls into a trancelike state from which she expounds the mysteries he's been puzzling over all his life. She speaks in the voice of a great Djinn, and each morning she rises in what he thinks is childish ignorance of all that has passed."

The streets were crowded with noon-time traffic. I was too tired to face taking Borges to that bench by the river and listening to him talk all afternoon. I drove around and around the same block to create the illusion of progress. In my exhaustion I could identify with the young bride in her trancelike state. I too had fallen into the clutches of a great

Djinn, and he wouldn't stop talking. Was I ever going to escape from this endless maze of Arabian tales?

"Yeats's wife was a kind of Scheherazade," he went on, "telling him tales to save her marriage if not her life. Perhaps that's why he married her, a much younger woman, not unlike the slave girls that Harun al-Rashid surrounded himself with: he needed her to tap into the spirit world that a poet must believe in whether it exists or not. The first weeks of their marriage were anxious, depressed, fraught with a growing sense that it had been a mistake. Then George Yeats—that was his wife's name, oddly enough: George, the same as my own—George Yeats discovered that if she held a pen in her hand and let it be guided by a force which, her husband believed, came from outside her, mirroring his preoccupation with archetypes that lived just beyond his reach, she could captivate him with the most outlandish inventions. He told himself that she was naive, that she didn't understand or even remember the tales she told him; that her tales were the work of an occult force. Of course he couldn't let himself see her as an illusionist: that would have broken the spell. He had to believe—the way a child has to believe in a fairy tale—that her inventions were real. This poem shows that in his heart he knew otherwise. He understood the bargain he had struck with his Scheherazade, and he worried that someday she would lose her innocence and perceive that he loved her for that midnight voice—which, of course, was something she already knew."

I pulled the car over into a shady spot and began to tell him that I had to go home.

"You see," he interrupted, "the game of love, like chess, is a game of strategy in plain view, a game of illusion.

Yeats knew that, though he pretended not to. Am I capable of this kind of heroic self-deception? Would I be brave enough to take a Scheherazade into my bed?"

He paused as if expecting answers to his questions. I tried to think of something to say that wouldn't be offensive. "You're married, of course."

"My marriage won't survive this trip," he said. "I intend to divorce my wife when we return to Argentina."

I felt sorry to hear that, though I'd never witnessed any tenderness between him and his wife. Señora Borges was a depressive, rigid woman who stood aloof from her husband's preoccupations and seemed perpetually at a loss for words. It was hard to imagine what bargain he had struck with her so late in life. Still, I didn't want either of them to be unhappy. I wanted Borges to know that people cared about him. "I've learned a great deal from you," I said.

"Then you will soon despise me," he said, "and later you will forget me."

"No, of course not. I'll never—"

"Every artist feels the ambivalence toward his teachers and predecessors that Bruno Eissler felt toward The Great Abdul." His tone made it clear that, even in posturing as the inevitable target of rebellion, he would tolerate no dissent. "You copy your master's illusions and usurp his place on the stage. Then with a wave of the hand you make him vanish like Houdini's elephant and proceed to the biggest illusion of all: the pretense that your tricks are utterly new. If you succeed, you'll have your own followers, your own imitators; you'll even have precursors. They'll mimic you like a jealous mirror. I am mimicking Borges, he is mimicking—"

"Wait a minute!" I objected, starting to laugh. "You *are* Borges!"

"Oh, yes, I forgot," he smiled. "How silly of me."

∞

At times Borges seemed to have a tenuous grip on his own identity. One morning in the coffee shop he made the mad claim that another writer—whose name he refused to reveal—had been impersonating him for many years. "The man's an impostor. He has counterfeited my personality and plagiarized every word I've ever written."

Was this a joke or a delusion? More likely the latter: he seemed dead serious. I recalled his sympathy for Isidro Pla, the mad Cuban who'd made similar accusations against him. "That must be unnerving," I said.

"We're all impostors," he shrugged. "We spend our lives impersonating selves we don't really have."

Why wasn't he more upset? I wondered. An impersonator sounded a lot like a mirror to me.

"Fortunately," he said, as if trying to reassure me, "I've been able to thwart my nemesis by turning his imposture back on itself. In every respect in which he has failed to imitate me, I have imitated him. As a result the two of us have become identical."

"Identical?"

"Do you know Leibniz's doctrine of the 'identity of indiscernibles'? If two things are exactly alike, they are the *same thing*. And that is what has happened to me and my impersonator: we have become the same man. His writings are my writings, his personality is my personality. I no longer envy his fame or his many awards: they are my fame and my awards."

By this time I was laughing out loud. Obviously Borges was having a joke at my expense.

"Some say he's here in Cambridge right now," he smiled, "living in an apartment just a few blocks from here. But clearly that's impossible." He threw up his hands in exaggerated disbelief. "How can the same man be in two places at once?"

Tom stops by every morning to check under the sink for further deterioration. He's cheerful, conscientious, even-tempered—and extremely good looking Ingrid and I are in agreement that he would make an ideal match for Gracie. I've asked Nilsa about this and she concurs. Tom was a rare find, whether or not we ever get through to the landlord.

I now realize that to search unsuccessfully for the landlord is the closest I will ever come to knowing anything about him. Yesterday I called the real estate company to follow up with the property manager, Ms. Sheila McCurdy. My call was routed to an attorney named John Scott who informed me that Ms. McCurdy is no longer with the company. The attorney wanted to know what Ms. McCurdy had told me.

"She said the landlord is a busy man with a lot on his mind," I replied, "but she'd be sure—"

"Let me make something crystal clear," John Scott interrupted. "Most rental properties are owned by corporations or limited partnerships, entities that don't exist in a physical sense—they're what we call legal fictions. Consequently they don't have knowledge or emotions. So if Ms. McCurdy implied that the landlord is a man—or a woman—or anything resembling the same, I apologize."

"Then if it's not a person—"

"Again, let me be clear. At the management company, we don't necessarily know who or what the landlord is. Our job is to collect the rent, deduct our commission, and forward the balance, in this case, to a post office box in Decatur, Illinois. The landlord itself, if it's a corporation or limited partnership, doesn't know what it is because it isn't anything."

"In any case, major repairs are the landlord's responsibility."

"Apartments in your building are rented on an as is/where is basis," he said. "Consequently there are no major repairs. Minor repairs are your responsibility."

I saw an opening. "If there are minor repairs, then there must be major repairs."

"Let's not play games." His tone was severe, almost hostile. "Who's to say—from the landlord's perspective—that there's even anything wrong with your pipe? Maybe it's *supposed* to leak? Did you ever think of that?"

My conversation with the lawyer made me realize how little I could ever hope to know about the landlord. It's easier to describe what the landlord *isn't* than to say what he is. He never comes to the building. He never talks to the tenants or even to the property manager. He has a lot on his mind, if he has a mind, and in any case he can't concern himself with every leaky pipe. For reasons known only to himself, he might even want the pipe to leak. So if I don't like raw sewage dripping in under the sink, I'm going to have to fix it myself.

Ingrid would rather put me in assisted living than see me lay a wrench on that pipe. I've tried to explain that finding the landlord will take forever, or at least a lot more time than I have left on my lease. Bringing her around to my point of view will take at least as long, but I won't stop trying. If nothing else, Borges taught me to have patience with infinity.

5.

The Force of Destiny

The superior man is quiet and calm, awaiting
his destiny, while the small man walks on
dangerous paths, trusting in cleverness and
luck.

Zisi (circa 481-402 BC),
Doctrine of the Mean

Evil isn't necessarily a bad thing."

I sipped my coffee, Borges his maté, as we
lounged in our usual booth at the coffee shop. I
wasn't in the mood for a philosophical debate. When we'd
walked in that morning, my heart had leapt to find Diotima
back on the job, the troll nowhere to be seen; but an hour
later, thanks to Borges, she had apparently come to the
conclusion that she'd rather fill salt shakers than risk eye
contact with me. Whenever I'd tried to turn on the charm,
whenever I'd had her smiling at me and laughing at my
jokes, whenever I'd come close to asking her for a date,
Borges would blurt out one of his paradoxes, demonstrating
conclusively, to the lights of any normal person, that the
two of us were stark raving mad. If I had a lingering shred
of hope, it evaporated when he launched into a dogged
defense of free will, declaring, just as Diotima stepped over
to refill my coffee cup, that evil isn't necessarily a bad thing;

she lowered her eyes and hurried away. I waited for a backward glance, a knowing wink, some recognition that I wasn't Borges and he wasn't me, but that gesture of absolution never came. Was I fated to spend the rest of my life without the woman I loved?

"For you see," Borges droned on, ignorant of my inner turmoil, "in a perfect world—a world without evil—nothing would ever change, because with change, inevitably, comes regret, or delight, and both of those emotions imply a less than perfect world. All emotion is predicated on change. In a perfect world there would be no emotion, no freedom, no creativity, no art. Only destiny."

"Even in a less than perfect world," I hesitated, "even in an evil world, there could still be destiny."

"I reject destiny. A poet must claim the right to make choices."

I walked over to the counter to pay the check. Diotima handed me my change without looking up. I left a more than usually generous tip on the table and helped Borges to his feet.

"What is evil?" he asked rhetorically as I guided him out the door. "Something we must resist at every turn. And what is the worst thing we can imagine? A world without evil."

An hour later we sat on a bench overlooking the Charles River, enjoying what promised to be a perfect Spring day. A giant sycamore loomed over us, sprouting a few green buds. A pair of white swans idled along the opposite bank. Evil was nowhere in sight.

A tall and breathtakingly beautiful young woman suddenly appeared in front of us, mounting the steep embankment as if she'd risen out of the water. She wore a red shawl over a black dress; her skin was pale, almost transparent. She had flowing blond hair and crystal blue eyes that seemed to stop time in its tracks.

"Señor Borges," she said, smiling. "I've been looking all over for you." She stepped forward as if to shake hands, though of course Borges wouldn't have shaken hands with a woman (he could barely bring himself to shake hands with a man), especially a beautiful woman who hailed him on the street. "Moira Hrafnsdóttir from the *Globe*. Could you spare a few minutes?"

I wondered if Borges had been expecting her. "Unfortunately not," he said, waving her away like an annoying insect. "This young man and I are discussing matters of the utmost importance."

"I'm doing a story on you," she said. "Featuring your exploits as a detective."

"Speak to the police," he said.

"I've called your office several times to arrange an interview. They've been completely uncooperative."

"I have no interest in being caught in your web of words."

"It's not a plot," she laughed. "It'll only take a few minutes. I just—"

"Speak to the police," he cut her off. "Unless you want me to call them myself."

She tilted her head and stared at Borges, probably trying to decide whether to take him seriously, though he'd been so rude that the answer should have been obvious. After a long moment she turned her gaze on me, and with a wry smile she handed me one of her business cards—"Just in case he changes his mind"—and disappeared down the jogging trail.

"She's very beautiful," I said as I watched her walk out of my life.

"I'm sure she is," Borges said. "Fortunately beauty can no longer seduce me."

It can still seduce me, I thought. I slipped her card into my breast pocket, the one closest to my heart.

"I wonder if she's aware of the meaning her Norse forbears would have attached to her name," Borges mused. "Hrafnsdóttir—the raven's daughter. Undoubtedly one of the mythical females who entangle men in the web of fate."

"Obviously you don't intend to let them entangle you."

"You can't escape them," he said. "No matter how much you try."

At Borges's apartment another surprise waited to entangle us. A Detective Freitag of the Cambridge Police, Homicide Division, sat in Borges's living room, enjoying a cup of tea with his wife. Detective Freitag was about fifty, bald, with drooping jowls, a pair of sunken eyes and more facial tics than an aging prizefighter. He was entertaining Señora Borges with the grisly details of a recent homicide, dramatized with a pantomime of twitches, stretches and squints. Señora Borges took the opportunity to practice some of the English phrases she'd studied in her Berlitz guide. "It is an honor and a privilege," she told Detective Freitag as we walked in, "to introduce you to my husband. Señor Borges; Detective Freitag of the Cambridge Police."

"Homicide Division," the detective added.

Borges bowed slightly. "To what do I owe this honor?"

Detective Freitag—in spite of his facial tics a more shrewd observer of men than the beautiful reporter had been—made no attempt to shake Borges's hand or to engage him in small talk. Instead, keeping a respectful distance, he cleared his massive throat and gave a succinct account of the reason for his visit. The police, he explained, had been so impressed with Borges's recent detective work that they were hoping he could help them solve a new murder case. A Scottish professor named MacIver Adamson had been found bludgeoned to death in Cambridge Common, a city park just three blocks away from Borges's apartment. Robbery was clearly not the motive, since the professor's wallet had been found on his body. Also found—and this suggested the real reason for the detective's visit—was Adamson's pocket calendar, which noted a lunch appointment with Borges during the previous week.

Detective Freitag puckered his lips and wobbled his head when he came to the end of the story. "Now what—speaking as a detective—do you make of that?" he asked Borges. "It's a strange coincidence, isn't it, that the man would be lunching with you just before he was murdered?"

"No stranger than most things," Borges smiled. "Everything that happens is a coincidence if you arbitrarily link it to something else."

"Arbitrarily!" the detective hooted, squinting out through laughing eyes. "You're right about that. Well—did he say anything, while you were having lunch, that sheds any light on his death? Did he seem worried or afraid?"

"Not at all."

For a moment Detective Freitag seemed to have lost his train of thought. "This professor must have been a good friend of yours," he finally said. "I mean, why else would you be having lunch with him? Although you don't seem too upset—not the least bit upset, in fact—to hear what happened to him."

"I knew him slightly," Borges said. "We had a minor business matter to discuss."

"And what was that, if I may ask?"

"A confidential matter of no relevance to his murder."

The detective lurched toward Borges and stared into his clouded eyes. "Where were you on Tuesday night? About eleven o'clock?"

"Here in my apartment, naturally. Where do suppose I was?"

"Are there any witnesses who could attest to that?"

"Am I a suspect, Detective? If not, then I must ask you to leave. It's nearly time for my lunch."

Detective Freitag picked up his hat and headed for the door, anxiously followed by Señora Borges, who understood nothing of what had been said. "I am so very pleased to have made your acquaintance, Detective Freitag," she said, extending her hand. "I hope that you will pay us the honor of a return visit."

"Oh, I will," the detective grinned. "You can depend on it."

Borges asked me to stay for lunch. His wife served tomato soup, smoked salmon and Russian salad while Borges talked nonstop about William James's essay on determinism. His tone of voice made it clear that no other topics would be discussed. I was shocked—as he must have known—to hear him feign ignorance and unconcern about Professor Adamson. I'd been present when they met for lunch, less than a week before, and had never seen Borges so emotional and overwrought. What was he hiding? Did he know more than he was willing to reveal about the professor's murder?

It had all started one morning as we sat in the coffee shop opening Borges's mail, which I'd just picked up at the post office. In addition to the usual junk mail there was a letter from Professor MacIver Adamson, of the University of Inverness, in Scotland, announcing his impending arrival in Boston and enclosing an article he'd recently published in the Journal of Comparative Latin American Literature. The article was about Borges; it purported to be a "biographical sketch" elaborating a Freudian interpretation of his life and work. Without ever talking to Borges, Adamson had analyzed some of his stories, not in terms of literary style or concept, but entirely based on the struggles and disappointments of Borges's personal life, particularly his relationships with women. The facts of Borges's life were well known. His father had died some thirty years before, and he continued living with his mother until his marriage, at the age of 68, shortly before his arrival in the United States. Naturally he'd had a few romances—and a few disappointments—during those bachelor years. Professor Adamson had extracted a handful of details from this sketchy history and concocted a Freudian explanation for Borges's most famous stories, based on a fancied interpretation of Borges's sex life or absence thereof, and speculation about his relationship with his mother.

Needless to say, Borges was furious. He hated Freud and bristled at the suggestion that psychoanalysis might have anything worthwhile to say about his work. In Borges's austere aesthetic, the personality of the artist was an irrelevancy. Art, to be worthy of the name, must be archetypal and absolute, not merely contingent or determined by the idiosyncrasies of any individual. Not that Borges himself was lacking in idiosyncrasies when it came to either the ego or the id, especially in regard to women. He spent forty-five minutes denouncing Professor Adamson in the most vivid terms, casting aspersions on his scholarship, his sanity and his nationality, and then, turning his prosecutorial eye on the professor's article, he tried, condemned and executed the Freudian approach to literature—on purely aesthetic grounds, without once mentioning any other reason he might have had to reject it, such as the Oedipus complex and what it implied for a man who'd remained single and lived with his mother until he was in his late sixties.

"Adamson's article is only the beginning," I told him, glancing again at the professor's letter. "He's planning to write a full-length biography based on the same methodology."

"I won't stand for this!"

"What are you going to do? Sue him? Have him dragged through the streets?"

"No," Borges said. A disingenuous smile spread over his face. "I'm going to invite him to lunch."

Adamson in person was even worse than Adamson in print. He was larger than life—at least six and a half feet tall—

with a full red beard, a crushing handshake and an insufferable way of smirking as he talked, as though he belonged to a more advanced species. Fortunately Borges couldn't see any of this, or the fisticuffs might have started before we sat down; but he could hear his voice, which droned out in a guttural brogue that might have been ideal for herding sheepdogs in the Scottish highlands, yet still managed to drip (if a voice can drip) with condescension. I braced myself for a bad case of indigestion.

We met at an upscale restaurant on Newbury Street called Fleur de Lys. It was the kind of place where the waiters hovered at ten-foot intervals with linen napkins draped over their arms, flitting up to the table periodically to whisk crumbs away from the plates. I ordered the closest thing they had to a hamburger, Borges requested something in French, and Adamson, after detailing the specifications of his filet mignon—"Warmed through, that is, red in the center, bright pink all round, barely browned on the edges"—demanded a 1954 Côtes du Rhône of which, the head waiter apologetically explained, there were only six bottles in existence. "In that case," Adamson relented, lowering his voice, "just bring me a glass of burgundy."

At first the conversation proceeded peacefully enough, with an exchange of gossip about the people Borges and Adamson knew in common, mostly scholars of Latin American literature. Adamson told some amusing anecdotes about his upbringing in Scotland, claiming kinship with David Hume and Robert Louis Stevenson, and Borges contributed a few observations about Duns Scotus and Lady Macbeth. Through the appetizers and the main course, they seemed to be dancing around the topic that had brought them together, until finally—it was just after the waiter had brought the coffee and dessert—they could avoid it no longer. Borges explained, in his most offensively polite tone of voice, that he objected to psychological analysis as a substitute for literary criticism. He added that he objected even more to psychological analysis as a substitute for biographical research. "Studying a writer's life for the light it sheds on his writings is a time honored— though, in my opinion, rather pedestrian—approach to literature," he said. "But what you seem to be doing, Professor Adamson, is much less defensible. You are attempting to reconstruct a writer's life from his writings."

"Yes, of course," Adamson said, scooping sugar into his coffee. "I'm writing a biography."

"Did I say less defensible?" Borges laid his knife and fork down beside his plate as if preparing for a dissection. "I should have said dishonest and completely unacceptable. You are using my writings to construct a narrative of my life that never took place."

"Naturally you would say that," Adamson smirked. "There are parts of your life you'd rather keep secret. Everyone has a few of those."

I was alarmed to see Borges reaching for his walking stick, which he often did when he was angry. "Speak for yourself, Professor."

"Did I mention that I studied to be a Freudian psychoanalyst?" Adamson laughed. "So you can't fool me, not about anything. I can see right through you."

A tremor shook the table as Borges rattled his walking stick against the edge. "I despise Freud and everything he stands for," he declared. "His cynicism, his reductionism, his monomaniacal obsession with sex—above all, his psychological determinism, his implicit denial of free will in every area of life, including art."

"Ah, yes!" Adamson scoffed. "Free will!"

"To apply his pseudo-scientific method to a human being is folly; to apply it to an artist is an outrage."

Adamson's smirk had expanded to a grin of almost simian proportions. I noticed for the first time how jagged and yellow his teeth were. "Your tirade against Freud stems from what we call denial," he said. "Particularly when it comes to what you label his obsession with sex."

"Denial?" Borges sputtered. "Sex? What are you talking about?"

"Masking an even deeper denial—so deep that you don't even mention it—of the Oedipus complex."

"Oedipus?" I heard the walking stick start to thump on the floor.

"Doesn't it seem sometimes that you're living a double life—one of self-consciousness, the other of self-delusion? Remember that Oedipus, acting out a curse he was not aware of, killed his father and married his mother—"

Borges cut him off. "What does Oedipus have to do with me?"

"Isn't it true that you've lived with your mother all your life? Until quite recently, in fact?"

A hush fell over the room as the waiters and other patrons began to sense the tension building at our table. Borges seemed suddenly absent, as if time had taken him backwards to a sultry night in the Buenos Aires of his youth, when such an insult would have led to a knife fight, if not an assassination. "After my father died," he said quietly, "I continued to live with my mother for many years. At first because she was dependent on me, later because I became dependent on her." He flicked a gnarled hand in front of his useless eyes. "Yes, I am blind, but unlike Oedipus I didn't pluck out my eyes because of an incestuous relationship with my mother. I suffer from a hereditary disorder which also left my father sightless before he died. And by the way, I didn't kill him."

"You have two selves," Adamson said, "like the most famous characters of your favorite writer—Dr. Jekyll and Mr. Hyde. Outwardly you're a mild-mannered gentleman, amusing your readers with ingenious paradoxes. But just below the surface lurks the mind of a killer. Call it determinism if you like; I call it human nature. No man can elude his destiny."

"This is an outrage!" Borges said, throwing his napkin down on the table.

"Volumes of evidence support my theory—your essays, your poems, your stories—and you're the author of all of it." Adamson shot a glance at me as if for confirmation of his bizarre accusations. "The cumulative effect, particularly of your stories, is overwhelming. They brim with murder: knife fights, duels, contrived executions. Are these just fantasies? Or thinly veiled autobiographical facts? Could the injury to your eyes have been self-inflicted? Could it be that you're a murderer—or wish you were, which, in psychoanalytic terms, amounts to the same thing? Is it possible that your father's death was not an accident?"

Borges's hand gripped the edge of the table. "My father died of heart disease."

"Do you expect me to believe that?"

Before I could stop him, Borges grabbed the walking stick and lurched to his feet. He staggered forward, stumbling into the table, and lashed the stick in front of him

like a blindfolded child lunging at a piñata. He missed
Adamson's head by a couple of inches. Adamson laughed
and ducked backwards.

"I insist that we settle this outside!" Borges hissed.

Adamson laughed again. "Did you bring your knife?"

"Gentlemen!" I said, stepping between them. "Let's
not get carried away! Please sit down!"

"I demand satisfaction!" Borges said.

"If by chance you didn't get an opportunity to kill your
father," Adamson baited him, "obviously you're still looking
for a substitute. Do you want to kill me?"

The eyes of everyone in the room were upon us. The
waiters had run for cover. "Please!" I begged. "Both of
you! Sit down!"

Borges muttered an imprecation in Spanish and let me
ease him back into his chair. I could feel his pulse racing as
I gripped his wrist. "We'll see what my readers think,"
Adamson smirked.

That remark sent Borges into a new fit of rage. He
tried to stand up but I pinned him down. "You wouldn't
dare publish such obscene speculations!"

"I will if I think they're true," Adamson said. "And it
seems likely that they are, though it's possible"—he held his
hand up as if to ward off another attack—"it's possible that
I could be convinced otherwise. Given the right incentives."

"Incentives?" Borges growled. "What do you mean?"

"Just what I said. Given the right incentives, I might
not jump so readily to conclusions that you find
objectionable."

Borges brooded for a full minute before he spoke
through clenched teeth: "Are you blackmailing me?"

"Oh, no, sir! Nothing like blackmail!" He chuckled as if Borges had made an outlandish suggestion. "I'm merely proposing that you and I have a more cooperative relationship. I'm going to write your biography, whether you like it or not. But if you give me full access to your personal papers, your letters, your diaries and notebooks, let me interview your mother, your sister—"

"Never!" Borges shouted. "You will never have access to that information!"

"In that case"—Adamson stood up and edged toward the exit, in case Borges attacked again—"it's clear what my biographical approach will be. I'll have no choice but to rely on the evidence contained in your writings."

The next morning Borges confessed over his pot of maté that after a night of soul searching he had concluded that Adamson was right. "I do want to kill him," he said with a bitter smile. "But unfortunately it's a physical impossibility, a locked room mystery in reverse: the would-be murderer is locked in a room by himself—that's what it's like to be a blind old man—and there's no way to get to the victim. Can you think of a solution?"

I laughed at what I took for a Borgesian irony—the idea that you would murder a man for the insult of calling you a murderer—and assumed that I'd heard the last of Professor Adamson. But a few days later Borges told me that Adamson had called on the telephone. Evidently he'd attended a reception at the Ibero-American Society, where he met Ronaldo Pérez, who had never forgiven Borges for that scathing review published in 1954. When Adamson mentioned his psychoanalytic theories about Borges, Pérez suggested that he speak with Renata Alarcón, who would tell him "everything he needed to know" about Borges. "Those were his words," Borges growled. "*Everything he needed to know! From that... harlot!*"

I remembered Renata Alarcón from the earlier reception at the Ibero-American Society. She was an aging Brazilian beauty, married to an unsavory Argentine wine exporter who looked like a hit man in a 1940s gangster movie. Hector Alarcón had been jealous and abusive toward Borges, which suggested a prior relationship between Borges and his wife, though I had a hard time imagining what it could have been. In any case, Borges didn't want Adamson talking to Renata about it. "I tried to warn Adamson about the Alarcóns," he told me. "They're gangsters who would knife a man for the price of their next drink, and slander him in the bargain. I said all this to Adamson, but the more I tried to dissuade him, the more eager he was to talk to them. I'm afraid my fervor against the Alarcóns must have signaled to Adamson that they'd provide him with plenty of evidence to use against me—as if, in some perverse way, I was luring him on."

Borges seemed anguished at the thought that he had driven Adamson to the Alarcóns. "Don't worry about it," I told him. "If they're that bad, Adamson's wasting his time. Nobody's going to believe a word those people say."

"You don't understand," Borges groaned. "I'm not afraid for myself. It's Adamson I'm worried about."

"Adamson?"

"They'll kill him. I'm almost certain that they'll kill him."

"Why would they do that?"

"They have their reasons." Clearly he was holding something back. I knew better than to try to pull it out of him.

"Did you tell Adamson you think the Alarcóns will kill him?" I asked.

"No, of course not."

"Why not?"

"Because he would demand an explanation I'm not prepared to give."

A few days after Borges's first visit from Detective Freitag, I found Moira Hrafnsdóttir's business card in my shirt pocket. It listed a phone number at the *Globe* where I could reach her or leave a message. Borges had treated her rudely and I wanted to apologize; it was the least I could do—or so I told myself. The truth was, I could hardly get Moira Hrafnsdóttir out of my mind. There was chemistry between us, at least on my side, and it was the kind of chemistry they build atomic bombs with. Did I dare call her? Somehow the question was tied up with Borges: I felt a mixture of shame and dread as I considered it, as if I were betraying him—even though, in theory, as long as I didn't talk about him it was none of his business. But face it: she'd given me the card in case he changed his mind about talking to her; she wasn't interested in me—all she'd do was pump me for information about Borges. I picked up the phone, dialed half the number, and stopped: I felt as if I were turning my father in to the secret police.

I crumpled the card, then straightened it back out and buried it in my wallet. I'd have the whole summer, I told myself, to follow up with Moira Hrafnsdóttir. Borges's year at Harvard was almost at an end.

In the meantime, his behavior had grown increasingly bizarre, as if he were playing a game of cat and mouse—or multi-dimensional chess—first with the Alarcóns, then with Adamson, and now with Detective Freitag. The chess analogy comes to mind because of a discussion we had one morning about William James's essay on determinism. James was not a fan of determinism, mostly for pragmatic reasons, though he admitted that on a large scale the determinists have a point. There is a sense in which the universe rolls on inexorably without regard to human actions or desires, but he asks us to envision the process as a game of chess between ourselves and the "infinite mind" in which the universe lies. We must play according to the rules—that is, according to the possible choices we are presented with—but within those limits we play freely. The universe bifurcates continuously as choices are made, but whichever branch of the bifurcations becomes real, the infinite mind knows what it will do at the next bifurcation to keep things from drifting away from the predetermined final result. "In other words," Borges said, "the outcome of the game is never in doubt. But each individual move is left to our choice and intelligence—with the knowledge, of course, that if we make a wrong move the game may be over sooner than we might have liked."

The time had come for Detective Freitag to make his next move. He had learned from the Harvard Spanish Department that on the night of Adamson's murder, Borges was not at home, as he had told him, but at Sanders Theater, several blocks away, delivering the last of his Charles Eliot Norton lectures. The detective had also visited the Fleur de Lys restaurant and been given a detailed account of Professor Adamson's lunch with Borges, including the unforgettable moment when Borges threatened him with his ivory-handled walking stick.

"I know nothing about this murder," Borges told the detective. "I don't even know how Adamson was killed."

"He was beaten to death with a long, blunt object," Freitag replied, staring down at Borges's walking stick. "Like a cane."

"Just a coincidence," Borges said.

"That's right," the detective scowled. "Everything's a coincidence, isn't it?"

"Obviously it would have been impossible for me to go outside, walk all the way to Cambridge Common by myself, and beat a man to death. Unless you think I drank a secret potion, like Dr. Jekyll."

The detective fixed his eyes on Señora Borges. "Then you must have had an accomplice."

Señora Borges misunderstood this remark, taking it as a compliment. "My accomplishments, they are nothing," she blushed. "For which you have my most humble thanks."

"I said 'accomplice!'" the detective barked. "Not 'accomplishments.'"

Borges gave him the kind of withering gaze that only a blind poet would dare to aim at a police officer. "If you are insinuating, sir, that my wife played a role in the crime you have been accusing me of," he said, struggling to his feet, "I must insist that we finish this outside."

It took the detective what seemed an eternity, punctuated by more than a few twitches, pouts and double takes, to realize that Borges was challenging him to a fight. And from there it was a short step to the realization that the poet had issued a challenge not only to his honor but to his credulity. If it was absurd to think of stepping outside with Borges for a tussle, how much more absurd was it to accuse him of clubbing the six-and-a-half foot tall Professor Adamson to death in a park three blocks away? The detective covered his discomfiture with a burst a raucous laughter. "All right, Señor," he said. "You win for now. But the minute I find the tiniest scrap of evidence that links you to Adamson's death, I'll be all over you like white on rice."

That last simile offended Borges even more than the insinuations against his wife. "Like white on rice?" he muttered after the detective had left. "Why is a man like that allowed to carry a gun?"

Late the next afternoon we sat in Borges's living room sipping dry sherry as Señora Borges, aided by two teenage boys from the neighborhood, bustled through the apartment packing clothes, books and papers into suitcases and steamer trunks and hauling them down to the curb. I didn't want to ask, because I wanted to be able to plead ignorance to Detective Freitag, but it seemed that the couple was planning a trip, possibly across the equator. In a few minutes, without a second thought, Borges would leave me with a lifetime of puzzles and enigmas, along with some practical issues about the most recent mystery that I needed to clear up.

"I can't help thinking of what you told me about the Alarcóns," I told him. "And how you were sure they would kill Adamson if he talked to them."

"Yes?" he sniffed, as if I had dredged up some old topic that was hardly worth remembering.

"Do you think they killed him?"

"Of course they killed him."

"Then why didn't you tell the police?   If they're accusing you, and you know who did it—"

"It's not as simple as that."

"Nothing is simple, is it?"

"No, I should hope that you've learned that by now." Borges sat sipping his sherry for a few minutes as we both listened to a pair of crows cawing in the tree that stood beside the building. It was a mild spring day and a delicious breeze drifted in through the open windows. Señora Borges could be heard in the next room instructing the teenagers in Edwardian English. "You've been working with me these past few months," Borges finally said, "so I suppose I owe you an explanation. But I'm telling you this on condition that you keep it to yourself. Is that agreed?"

"Agreed," I agreed.

"After you and I last spoke about Adamson, I spent three sleepless nights agonizing about the position I'd put him in. I had tried to persuade him not to meet with the Alarcóns, and that only made him more determined to see them. There was a way to save him, I knew, but I hated the idea of doing what it required. Finally I realized I had no choice: I couldn't just let the man die. I phoned him and agreed to give him access to all the letters and other documents he needed for his biography, as he'd demanded, if he would have nothing more to do with the Alarcóns. I didn't know I was inadvertently pushing him to his death. It was my efforts to prevent his murder that brought it about."

Was this really true? I wondered. Or was it just another Borgesian conceit? "I don't understand," I said.

"I haven't finished yet." His tone of voice suggested that he'd sensed my skepticism masked as lack of understanding. "In his first call to Renata Alarcón," he went on, somewhat tartly, "Adamson must have told her just enough to give her the impression that he knew some things about Jorge Luis Borges that are not generally known. I don't intend to tell you the nature of those secrets. Let me just say that they relate to certain facts of a personal nature—not the hideous crimes Adamson accused me of—and the Alarcóns have been basing their livelihood on their knowledge of those secrets for many years."

I could hardly believe what he was telling me. "Have the Alarcóns been blackmailing you?"

"We won't discuss it further," he said, waving my question away. "Adamson, in his stupid self-importance, must have said something to Renata Alarcón that suggested he knew the secret—which in fact he did not—and he must have mentioned that he was writing a biography. She and her gangster husband perceived that they would be out of business if Adamson went public with this information. They agreed to meet with him, hoping to find out what he knew. And when he called them back—after I'd convinced him to avoid them—and canceled the meeting, they tracked him down three blocks from my apartment and bludgeoned him to death."

Borges set down his sherry glass and sighed. The crows answered with a chorus of jeers. I had the feeling that there was more to the story that what he'd told me. "Well, you've solved the crime," I said.

"Unfortunately, yes," Borges said. "And it's the last crime I'll ever attempt to solve."

"Why do you say that? All you have to do is tell the police—"

"The die is cast. I have no choice but to accept my destiny." He pushed himself into a standing position with his walking stick and asked me to help him put his suit jacket on. When I'd done that, I brushed off some lint that had accumulated on the lapel. "You heard Adamson that day at the Fleur de Lys," he went on, straightening his tie, "when he demanded 'incentives' for not writing his libelous biography. He was blackmailing me for being a murderer— he wanted to prove that, like Oedipus, I'd murdered my father—but the only person I ever murdered, as it turned out, was Adamson himself. So in effect he blackmailed me for his own murder."

"How can you say that?"

"He canceled the meeting with the Alarcóns at my insistence, and that was why they killed him."

"That doesn't mean you murdered him. In fact you were trying to protect him."

"Oedipus killed his father only because of the attempt to thwart his destiny, and so it was with me. It was Adamson's destiny to die, and mine to kill him."

Evidently it was time to go. I took his elbow and escorted him toward the door. "I thought you didn't believe in destiny," I said.

"I was wrong," he smiled. "Sometimes the victim of blackmail will have no choice but to commit the crime he is being blackmailed for. And likewise, for a detective, in some instances the solution causes the crime. In this case I solved the crime before it was committed, and my solution caused it to happen."

We stood in the open doorway, facing the staircase to the ground floor. The teenagers clambered up and down the stairs, shouting as they hauled the suitcases and trunks down to the street. Borges leaned on his walking stick, listening to the teenagers and the sounds coming in from the street and the open windows in the rooms behind him. He said, "If there's such a thing as destiny—as I now believe there is—then the whole process of the universe from the beginning of time is a single event. There's no cause and effect, just different parts of the same process. Does one thing cause another? You might as well say that one end of my walking stick causes the other."

"Everything goes in circles," I said, for lack of anything better to say.

"Something like that," he agreed. "The only way you can cheat destiny is to become someone else, like those pseudo-Arabian illusionists we came to know. They had a pretty good arrangement, didn't they, exchanging identities as the need arose? That's all I can do now—let the other fellow take over, the one who writes the stories and poems. His pages won't save me; eventually they won't save him either. Anyway I'm free of him now."

What was he talking about?

We stepped out on the landing to wait for Señora Borges. One of the neighbors cracked open her door and squinted disapprovingly at the teenagers. "Another thing I'm done with is pretending to be a detective," Borges said. "Each of us, in his own way, tries to solve the mystery of his existence. But search as we might, we can never find more than a few clues, and those lead in different directions, revealing other clues which, in turn, divide and take us down diverging paths. And so the more cunning and skill we exercise as detectives, the farther we get from the truth."

In the background I could hear Señora Borges shouting into the telephone: "I beg your pardon, sir. Would you be so kind as to send a taxicab to the following address?"

"I believe my wife is calling for a taxi," Borges said.

"I can take you," I said. "Wherever you're going."

"No, I'm afraid you can't." He shook his head and smiled at me for the last time. "You're on your own now."

Ten minutes later I watched Borges and his wife climb into a taxi and drive away. They didn't say where they were going and I didn't ask. Almost before the cab was out of sight I felt the presence of Moira Hrafnsdóttir beside me on the curb. I had no idea how she got there.

"They're gone, aren't they?" she asked, measuring my disappointment with her crystal blue eyes.

I nodded without turning to face her. "Do you want to go for a walk?" I felt better with her walking beside me than with the two of us staring at each other on the curb.

It was as if we'd been friends for a long time. We wandered toward the river and crossed Memorial Drive to the jogging path along the Charles River where we'd first met. Hordes of joggers, dog walkers, mothers with strollers and toddlers all competed to take advantage of the spring weather, surging past us and on around a bend or across the next bridge. We walked until we found a vacant bench under a sycamore still almost bare of leaves. It was the same bench where I'd sat with Borges the day she stepped over the embankment and introduced herself. We gazed out over the river, which looked the same as it always looked. A rowing team flashed by, cowering under an invisible lash. We talked about random things: the weather, politics, my graduate program, her job. Neither of us mentioned Borges.

"Nick," she finally said. "There's something you need to know. Since I've been working on this Borges article, it's been like I wandered into a hall of mirrors."

"I know the feeling."

"Not quite like this."

There was something new in her eyes, something skeptical, playful and at the same time inquisitorial. I reminded myself that she was an investigative reporter. "You worked on the magician case, right?" she asked. "The Great Abdul? You were there with Borges at the inquest?"

"Yes."

"Well, what would you say if I told you that on that very same day he was down in Connecticut giving a lecture at Wesleyan?"

I couldn't help laughing. "I'd say you've got the date wrong."

"That's what I assumed. But then I got a call from a Detective Freitag of the Cambridge police about another case—the Adamson murder that's been in the headlines lately. The detective had heard about the story I've been writing and he wanted to compare notes. He said Borges claimed he spent the night at home with his wife the night of the murder—that was his alibi, wasn't it? But the head of the Spanish Department told Freitag that Borges was at Sanders Theater until after ten o'clock, delivering the last of his Charles Eliot Norton lectures."

"Borges doesn't like Freitag. He might have lied to him on general principles. In any case he would have been back in his apartment by the time Adamson was killed."

"That's right," she said. "Three blocks from the crime scene."

I turned to face her, hoping to see a glimmer of irony in her eyes. She had the most serious face I'd ever seen, immobile and transparently white, as if it had been hewn out of ice. Not that she was cold—no, it was just that her flame burned steady and white. Nothing was ever going to deflect it.

"You don't really think he did it, do you?" I laughed. "He can hardly walk across the room without holding on to somebody's hand."

She raised her eyebrows. "Where were you that night?"

"Are you kidding me? I was up in Ipswich, watching TV." It was a lame alibi, but it was true. "Seriously, that's what I do most of the time."

The questions started coming one after the other. "Why didn't you go to the lecture?" she asked.

"Borges kept me insulated from his activities at Harvard. He didn't want me to attend his public lectures. They assigned a guy named John Murchison to help him with those."

"Did you ever meet Murchison?"

"No."

"What about Norman Thomas di Giovanni? The department head told me Borges has been spending most of his time with him, working on translations."

"He never mentioned him."

I leaned back and took a deep breath. My pulse was racing like a hamster on a wheel. Though I had nothing to hide, my first experience with an investigative reporter had triggered symptoms of panic and flight. I wanted to leap up and disappear into the passing stampede of joggers, hopefully ending up where no one would ever find me.

Moira Hrafnsdóttir peered at me with a look of anxious satisfaction. She ventured a smile. "OK," she said, "are you getting the picture? You've been hanging out with Borges for six months but you've never been to Harvard with him, or to any of his public lectures, and you've never heard of the people who've been taking him around. Is that it?"

"Something like that."

"Just roaming the countryside, solving murders?"

"No," I objected. "We've spent a lot of time in a coffee shop in Somerville."

"And at the same time Borges was solving murders, he was out giving lectures all over New England. The man must really be a genius."

"He is."

She nodded, lips puckered, as if considering all the evidence. "You know what? Even a genius can't be in two places at once."

"All right," I said. "Where are you going with this?"

Her serious face acknowledged that she owed me an answer. "Nick, I like you, so I'm going to tell you what I think. But you're the only person I'm going to tell, and only if you promise to keep it to yourself. Not a word, promise?"

"Mum's the word," I agreed.

"I don't think the man who just rode off in that taxi is really Jorge Luis Borges. The real Borges is painfully shy. He doesn't hang out at coffee shops or go around solving murders. He doesn't even like to give lectures. He's probably over at Harvard right now, having a quiet lunch with John Murchison or working on a translation with Norman Thomas di Giovanni."

"And... the man I've been hanging around with?"

"I think he's an impostor."

When Moira Hrafnsdóttir reached this conclusion—which, I realized, she'd been leading up to the whole time, taking care not to spring it on me all at once—I felt shaky, as though the earth might open and swallow me up. I was dazed with incredulity, but at the same time I experienced a sense of déjà vu that convinced me she was right. I remembered the pseudo-Arabian illusionists and what Borges had said about them as he was about to disappear from my life: "*They had a pretty good arrangement, didn't they—exchanging identities as the need arose?*"

I stood up and Moira Hrafnsdóttir walked with me along the river to the footbridge that crosses to the business school. We bought Cokes and hot dogs from a vendor and stood on the bridge watching the sun set through the gathering mist. Swallows swooped down in front of us, plucking flies out of the air near the water, then circling back into the sky before they swooped down again. What would it be like to be one of those flies? I wondered. You catch the eye of some swallow circling over the river; fatally, it swoops down at you—you're doomed—but in the last instant you dart over and change places with another fly, which is snatched up in your place. That's the best you're ever going to do.

"Moira—"

"I go by Katie," she smiled.

I laughed at the idea of a nickname so unlike her real name: Katie and Moira were the names of two different people. "That first day we met you," I said, "Borges and I, we were sitting on that same bench and you came up the embankment as if you were rising out of the mist. Borges wondered if you were one of those mythical creatures who entangle men in the web of fate."

She tossed her blond hair back and laughed. "My parents came from Iceland."

Then I told her the whole tale of my last six months from start to finish, from the day Cliff Jensen asked me to drive down and bring Borges up to Ipswich—for the purpose, as it turned out, of solving Howard Vaughan's murder, which had yet to be committed, and sending Cliff to prison for the rest of his life—to that mild April afternoon when Borges disappeared into a taxi, leaving me to my fate.

"Nick," Katie said gently, "he wasn't really Borges. He was an impostor."

"Whatever," I shrugged. "You know what he said this afternoon? 'The only way to cheat destiny is to become someone else.'"

She laughed again. "Well, that's what I'm going to have to do before I meet with my editor. I've spent the last six weeks writing a series of articles about the wrong man. No wonder the head of the Spanish Department looked at me like I was crazy."

"Think of poor Adamson," I brooded. "He was writing a whole biography about the wrong man—and it got him killed."

"Do you know who killed him?"

"A couple of gangsters who were blackmailing the wrong man."

She shook her head and touched my arm. "It's sad to think there's such evil in the world."

I had to agree. "But on the other hand," I said, cheering up, "if things hadn't happened just as they did—if Borges hadn't denied destiny and Adamson hadn't been killed and there wasn't evil in the world—then you and I wouldn't be standing here watching the sunset fade through the mist." I put my arm around her shoulders, and as I pulled her toward me, I caught a glimpse of that sunset reflected in her keen blue eyes. It was a more beautiful sunset than I'd ever seen before.

"I guess it was meant to be," she said.

∞

When Borges left me standing on that curb, something he'd said a few weeks before began to make sense. We'd been talking about Dante, and it startled me to hear Borges characterize himself as Virgil guiding me through the Inferno. Yes, we'd spent six months bringing poetic justice to a landscape fairly sizzling with evildoers, where every crime found its victim and the punishment always fit the crime. Howard Vaughan was abusive to his subordinates, so he'd been stabbed in the back by his most loyal lieutenant. Cliff Jensen concealed the murder and flaunted his learning; only Borges's greater learning could unmask him. Dr. Corwin, the psychiatrist who played God, was undone by a patient who raised the voices of the dead to accuse him. The over-inquisitive Professor Adamson (who counted as one of the criminals in Borges's scheme of things) had threatened Borges with a Freudian biography; not surprisingly he lost his life to a pair of blackmailers who beat him at his own game. No doubt we'd seen a slice of Hell right here in Massachusetts—but didn't Borges have our roles reversed? Hadn't I been leading him by the hand for the past six months, listening to him, humoring him, driving him wherever he wanted to go? No, he made it clear: the infernal journey had been mine. He was the guide and I was the pilgrim—and now I was on my own.

Years later, when I began to record these adventures, I understood how right he had been. By then I'd read most of his stories and some of the books he pointed me to, few of which I'd read at the time. But most of what I've learned hasn't come out of books. Truth be told, I wasn't much of a student. My idea of Comparative Literature, even in graduate school, was skimming Cliff Notes while watching daytime TV. That spring I missed too many classes and too many meetings with my new advisor, who blamed me for sending his predecessor to jail. The department dropped me at the end of the semester, and I took a job selling ice cream on the Boston Common, followed by stints driving a delivery truck, winding tapes in an audio products factory, and pushing clothes racks through howling throngs of harpies in Filene's Basement. A thorough knowledge of Dante's *Inferno* was indispensable for the full appreciation of my new life, or so I believed (based on the Cliff Notes). In a few months I received an invitation from my local draft board and began a brief military career, distinguished only by boredom, fear and occasional outbursts of violence. That was when I really saw Hell and earned my permanent place in it.

It was a time when young men my age were being called upon to make a choice, and all the choices were bad ones. More than once I thought of Borges during those tense last weeks when the machinations of Adamson and the Alarcóns had brought him to the edge of emotional collapse. One morning Señora Borges called in a panic and summoned me to their apartment, where Borges was in the midst of a crisis she couldn't understand: the crisis leading up to his surrender to destiny and his simultaneous attempt to escape from it. Some of his most cherished beliefs—

particularly monism and idealism, with their undercurrent of determinism—were locked in mortal combat with his lifelong dedication to freedom. I found him hunched over in his chair, sweating in his suit and tie, arguing with himself and clenching his hands together as if he wanted to strangle his opponent. "An old man is supposed to go quietly," he muttered when I sat down across from him and said hello, "like a soldier being sent to the front; to accept his fate in the name of a higher good. But as an artist and as a man— which amount to the same thing, since art is always about justice and morality—I demand the ability to make free choices! This means that evil must be permitted to exist in the world I inhabit. I can combat it—I must combat it— but I can't wish it out of existence, or I would lose my freedom." He leaned forward and scowled at me as if I were challenging him. "Does that make me a collaborator with evil? Let me ask you: Are you willing to trade your freedom for a world where every choice has already been made? The man who believes in destiny, like the God of the Puritans, must consent to every evil."

"Maybe I should come back later," I suggested. "It sounds like you're having another dark night of the soul."

"You can't escape," he said, shaking his head. "Evil, in effect, is our destiny."

When I got out of the Army, I stopped at the coffee shop in Somerville and asked about Diotima. The troll refused to give any account of her whereabouts and threatened to have me arrested if I ever set foot in the place again. But thanks to Borges I had met my destiny: Moira Hrafnsdóttir— Katie—the woman who would guide me for the rest of her life. I found her still writing for the *Globe* and eager to move on to something more challenging, such as marrying me. Did I say she was my destiny? I know better than that now—love, like everything else that makes life worth living, must be chosen freely. Now Katie's gone and I have Ingrid and Gracie, who worry about me day and night and torment me with their questions and reminders, as if I had no thought or memory of my own, and I love them for it. I may also have a landlord, though I've been unable to find him.

For a while I thought I also had Nilsa—sweet Nilsa!—but that was an old man's folly. The look of love was in her eyes, but it wasn't meant for me. It was for Tom—which explained her faithful attendance on my aching back and his protracted but ineffectual efforts to improve my plumbing. On the day I realized that, I released Nilsa from my dreams. I sent her down to Tom's apartment on some pretext, and she never came back. The two of them are together now and I wish them all the happiness in the world. Gracie will have to keep waiting for her prince, and I'll stay faithful to my memories of Katie.

Those memories begin on the bench overlooking the Charles River where I caught my first glimpse of her—and where, almost a year later, I saw Borges (or thought I saw him) for the last time. Spinning up Memorial Drive in the Galaxie, I glanced to my left and noticed an old man perched on that bench who bore an uncanny resemblance to Borges. I quickly parked the car and walked back up the path along the river, but by the time I reached the bench the old man I'd taken for Borges had disappeared. In his place sat a much younger man, as tall as Borges and bespectacled but with clear, watchful eyes and a shock of dark, wavy hair.

He shoved something into his pocket and glared at me for interrupting his solitude.

As for the man I chauffeured around for six months—what to make of him? I still think of him as Borges, even though he denied it in the end. In retrospect there was a lot of evidence for Katie's theory that the man I knew was an impostor. His refusal to spend his time at Harvard, his ban on photography, even his avoidance of mirrors; the women from his past—Scheherazade and Renata Alarcón—who seemed to hold some strange power over him; the unnamable nemesis he blamed for plagiarizing his identity and his works; and of course the many cryptic remarks that made no sense at the time. But all of these clues could have been deliberately planted and manipulated. It would be just like the real Borges, wouldn't it, to pass himself off as an impostor? It would be just like the real Borges to hire someone to impersonate him and do all the things he didn't want to do—such as lecturing at Harvard—so he could roam the New England countryside and sip maté in a coffee shop and solve crimes that no one else could solve; and it would also be just like him, even if he didn't hire an impersonator, to allow one to spring up from the shadows of his persona, the way Chung Ling Soo had imitated his master and eventually replaced him. In a world of facing mirrors, all explanations are equally possible.

Borges himself—the real Borges, if there was one—believed that personality and individual identity are an illusion. If he was right about that, then Katie may have been right about Borges, and Ingrid may be right about me. Maybe the Borges I knew never existed, except in my own mind.

Did I dream Borges, or did he dream me?

Final Author's Note

The ingenious gentleman known to Nick Martin as "Borges" was undoubtedly an impostor, if not a figment of his own imagination. With the end of this book he disappears from literary history, to return only if Mr. Martin sees fit to recount any further adventures. In the meantime I commend the reader to the real Jorge Luis Borges, who was of course the original of the "Borges" in this book and the author of the stories and essays claimed to have been written by him. If the reader takes nothing away from this book but a desire to read those stories and essays—particularly "Death and the Compass," "The Garden of Forking Paths," "The Library of Babel," "A New Refutation of Time" and "The Perpetual Race of Achilles and the Tortoise" (all published in English translation by Penguin Books), I will have accomplished my purpose.

About the Author

Bruce Hartman lives with his wife in Philadelphia. His previous books include *The Rules of Dreaming* (published by Swallow Tail Press in 2013), *The Muse of Violence* (2013), and *Perfectly Healthy Man Drops Dead* (Salvo Press, 2008). For more information, please see his website and blog, www.brucehartmanbooks.com.

Kirkus Reviews awarded *The Rules of Dreaming* its Kirkus Star for Books of Exceptional Merit and selected it as one of the "Top 100 Indie Books of 2013." *Kirkus* called the book, "A mind-bending marriage of ambitious literary theory and classic murder mystery... An exciting, original take on the literary mystery genre."

Made in the USA
San Bernardino, CA
04 February 2019